SYLVIA McNICOLL

FITZHENRY & WHITESIDE

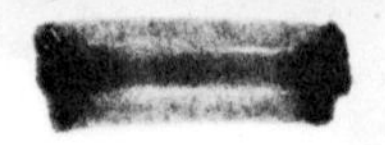

Published in Canada by Fitzhenry & Whiteside,
195 Allstate Parkway, Markham, Ontario L3R 4T8

Published in the United States by Fitzhenry & Whiteside,
311 Washington Street, Brighton, Massachusetts 02135

www.fitzhenry.ca godwit@fitzhenry.ca

10 9 8 7 6 5 4 3 2 1

Library and Archives Canada Cataloguing in Publication
McNicoll, Sylvia, 1954-
Beauty returns / Sylvia McNicoll.
ISBN 1-55005-100-8 (pbk.)
ISBN 1-55005-149-0 (bound).
1. Guide dogs—Juvenile fiction. I. Title.
PS8575.N52B42 2006 jC813'.54 C2006-900883-3

U.S. Publisher Cataloging-in-Publication Data
(Library of Congress Standards)

McNicoll, Sylvia, 1954-
Beauty returns / Sylvia McNicoll.
[208] p. : cm.
Summary: A contemporary high school love story: a girl who raises dog guides struggles to overcome the objections of her family, her friends, and her school, while she builds a relationship with an older blind and diabetic boy who is the new owner of one of her dogs.
ISBN 1-55005-149-0
ISBN 1-55005-100-8 (pbk.)
1. Guide dogs — Juvenile fiction. 2. Human-animal relationships — Juvenile fiction. 3. Labrador retriever — Fiction. I. Title.
[Fic] dc22 PZ7.M2385Bea 2006

Fitzhenry & Whiteside acknowledges with thanks the Canada Council for the Arts, and the Ontario Arts Council for their support of our publishing program. We acknowledge the financial support of the Government of Canada through the Book Publishing Industry Development Program (BPIDP) for our publishing activities.

Canada Council for the Arts   Conseil des Arts du Canada

Cover image by Sharif Tarabay
Design by Wycliffe Smith Design Inc.
Printed in Canada

Dedication

To Magic, the real dog guide; and all the other dogs, trainers, foster owners, and donors who make the real magic possible.

Acknowledgement

For all the help and information on foster puppies, thank you to Natalie Ann Comeau at Lions Foundation of Canada, Dog Guides. For guidance on the medical issues, thank you to Dr. Lindsay MacVicar. For generously sharing innermost thoughts and feelings about diabetes, blindness, dog guides, and life in general, thanks to Angela Mackay.

For more Information

For any of you who may wish for more information on dog guides, or how to donate or foster a puppy, please visit www.dogguides.com.

Chapter 1

Elizabeth Alone

"No steady boyfriends this year!" Alicia raises her hand to do a high five, curving her fingers back so as not to wreck her freshly-painted nails.

"We're playing the field!" I agree, touching my palm to hers carefully.

We squeeze together in front of the full-length mirror on my bedroom door. Alicia got her braces off in August, and she's blond and cute, with bubbly curls twisted and tacked on top of her head with a blue pencil. She's wearing blue sandals that match her toes and fingernails, and they have high cork platforms—so she's as tall as a fashion model.

I grew four centimetres taller and a cup size larger over the summer—and I still look short and young next to her. I've got a round face with freckles, which we've hidden with cover-up, and white eyelashes, which we've coloured with mascara. I'm wearing all one colour, cream, so as not to break the height I have. And once I iron my springy red hair, I'll look almost as cute as Alicia. Eat your hearts out, guys!

"You wasted far too much time moping about Scott last year." Alicia leans closer to the mirror and rubs some lipstick from her front teeth.

"And you did, too, with..." I list her boyfriends on my fingers (she was always chasing some guy), "Todd, Brant, Eric, Malcolm..."

"Enough already, you made your point. Do these jeans make me look fat?" Alicia straightens again and turns to check out her backside in the mirror.

"Nothing makes you look fat!" I tell her, checking my own backside, which looks bigger than hers. "And you're not changing again."

"Mmm, okay." She frowns, studying her left profile. Straight nose, perfect skin, no more overbite—what did she have to frown about?

"Did you hear Scott broke off with Gwen?"

I shake my head. "And I don't care, either!"

Surprisingly, it's true. I put my fist to my chest. There's no instant ache at the mention of his name. I dated him last summer, but I'm just totally over him.

"No one will ever make me feel that bad again." I sigh happily. Still, in the back of my mind, a little voice whispers something. I can't quite hear it—and it turns into a nagging hum.

Alicia squints at me. "Maybe I should call Scott. You don't mind, do you?"

"Alicia! Remember, no steady boyfriends this year. Casual or group dates only!" The nagging hum grows louder and clearer. I'm over Scott and don't care that he didn't call, but Kyle didn't call over the summer either, and that bothers me. Why, I don't know—it's what boys always do, promise to call and then don't.

"You're right. Scott has always been trouble for us." Alicia checks out her right profile in the mirror. "Your outfit looks great!"

"Thanks." We shopped for it together—of course Alicia likes it.

Mom thought I was nuts when I brought home light-coloured tee shirts and cargoes. "White? You bought white for the fall?" she said.

"It's winter white, Mom. Don't you think it goes well with my colouring?" I held the top up close to my face, which can look kind of orange when my freckles are really in bloom.

"Yes, but it's so impractical. You'll never be able keep that outfit clean."

Mom wears drabby clothes so that no dirt ever shows—what does she know? The mono-colour look is different, special. My belly button feels a bit cool, so I tug at the top to close the gap between it and my cargoes.

"We're done here. Let's go downstairs. I want to straighten my hair."

"Wait! The final touch." Alicia takes a small bottle from her backpack: Boy Catcher, the label says. She sprays herself for about thirty seconds, head to toe, until she smells like apple pie. "Want some?"

I sneeze and shake my head. Alicia stuffs the Boy Catcher back in her bag, along with all the clothes she's brought to try on. We high-step over last week's supply of my clothes, spread everywhere and into the hall. We follow bacon smells into the kitchen.

"To the laundry room," I tell her.

She clatters down the steps behind me to the all-purpose TV/computer/laundry room. I pick my way around the plastic rattles and wooden blocks on the floor to where the board and iron are standing, close behind the computer. I plug the iron in and wrinkle my nose at a really bad smell hanging in the air.

"Peek-a-boo, baby!" Alicia calls as she stumbles over a choo-choo push toy.

My sister's eight-month-old son sticks his head out from his room. All four of his teeth show, jack-o'-lantern style. Then he stuffs his juice bottle in his mouth and begins his creep across the orange nylon carpet towards us.

Dad renovated the basement last year. He added two rooms—one for my sister Debra and the other for Baby

Teal, although the two of them have pretty much taken over every room of the house—and everyone's lives. I roll my eyes and touch my spit-moistened finger to the iron. *Sish!* Lowering my head to the Teflon ironing-board cover, I spread my curls out and begin to iron.

"Debra showed me this trick. It makes my hair smooth."

"Where is your sister, anyway?" Alicia asks, and Mom emerges from Teal's room.

"Oh, hi, Mrs. Kerr."

"Shh, Debra's sleeping." My mother wipes baby drool from her brown top. "She was up half the night with the baby."

"Like anyone else could sleep, either," I grumble as I drape another section of my hair across the ironing board. No one listens. Since the baby arrived, I've become totally invisible unless somebody needs something.

The brat uses our wrecked old couch to pull himself up.

"You can stand up all by yourself. Aren't you the cleverest boy?" Alicia claps her hands with delight.

Hand over hand, Teal makes his way across the brown plaid cushions, drooling red juice from both corners of his mouth. The bad smell grows stronger as he gets closer.

I press the back section of my hair, keeping an eye on him. He's coming my way. When I finish pressing, I stand up.

"Check it out, Alicia, did I miss any parts?"

"No—wow! Your hair looks longer, too." She reaches out and touches it. That's why I don't quite register that Teal is making his break from the couch. A wobbly half step—and a tiny hand reaches out and grabs my pant leg. Then a drool covered mouth bites my knee.

"Ouch!" I yank my leg away, throwing the baby off balance. He wails in shock as he topples back. He's left two sets of juice prints on my pant leg.

"Crap! Mom—look! My brand new pants are ruined."

"Oh for heaven's sakes—just run some cold water over the spot." My mother's lips purse with disapproval.

"You honestly think you can get this red stuff out?"

Teal pulls himself up on the couch again and stretches one arm out toward me.

"Oh, no, you don't." I back up, and he cries.

"Elizabeth!"

What is it about my family? I'm the one with goo on my pants, and yet I'm the one in trouble.

"Is it too much to ask for? Clean clothes on my first day of high school?" I throw my hands up in the air. "And have you had a whiff of this child lately?"

Mom rolls her eyes. "I'm late for class. You change him this time. And don't forget to put away the ironing board. We have a baby in the house." She stomps up the stairs.

"What about my stain?" I call after her—no answer.

"We have a baby in the house." No kidding. I sigh.

Wisps of red hair stand up from his head like little question marks. Large honey-coloured eyes stare back at me—puppy-dog eyes that remind me of my second foster dog, Beauty. It's the expression they have most in common—accepting and trusting, yet totally baffled by the world around them.

"Don't look at me like that!" I lift Teal up but keep him at arm's length, holding my breath and wincing.

Alicia folds her arms across her chest and grins at me. She's not going to lift a finger, obviously. She wants to watch me get covered in crap. Heh, heh, I'll show everyone. "Time to wake up Mommy! She's had enough time to sleep, don't you think?" Teal still dangles from my hands as I kick open Debra's bedroom door.

Deb groans awake, sits up, and rubs her swollen eyes. Her black hair sticks up all over, porcupine style. "What time is it?"

"Eight fifteen. Everyone's late, and Teal's made a stinky."

"I need to take a shower. Can you just..."

"No."

As I lean over to dump him on the bed, Teal squirms and kicks. For a moment, I lose my footing and stumble, my chest on his face. He giggles as I pick myself up again.

"C'mon, Alicia, we're outta here!"

We take the stairs two at a time. Back in the kitchen, I

dab a wet washcloth at the red half moons on the knee of my cargoes. The half moons turn pink, then merge into a full moon. Who knows what the blob will look like when it dries again?

I throw on a jacket and grab my backpack. "Gotta go, Mom. Bye."

"Wait. Where's Teal?" Mom follows close at our heels, with her book bag in hand.

"Oh, Deb woke up just in time." We step out the door and Mom turns to lock up.

"Come straight home," she says, tucking her key into her purse. "We're going to Canine Vision Canada today."

"Really?" I grin. "You didn't tell me. What are we getting? Another Lab?"

I secretly hope so. Then it will be like my other dogs, Beauty I and II—like I hadn't given them away at all.

"A Golden Retriever. And I have a surprise for you." Mom climbs into the van, mumble, mumble, "...Magic." The door slams shut.

"What's that? The new dog is magic?" Too late, Mom's already backing the van up. Alicia and I continue to school.

The leaves still dance on the branches in their summer greens, and the sun beams down, white-hot, across my back and shoulders. It doesn't seem like autumn at all, and for sure it's too hot for the first day of school. I take off my jacket and sling it over one shoulder.

"Elizabeth, what's that? You've got a red mark on your right boob." Alicia points and chuckles.

She's right. There's a perfect little red O circling where my nipple is located, a couple of layers down.

"Juice drool. Drat, that kid ruins anything. Got something in your collection I can wear over this?"

She opens her bag and rifles through, pitching me a green tee shirt.

"Hurry up," Alicia says.

I yank it over my head and push my arms through the sleeves. Not the mature monochromatic effect I hoped for—still, it hides the stain.

The sidewalks are deserted as we approach the school, a sure sign the first bell has rung.

"Look, it's one of those new Statuses." Alicia points to a black SUV stopped in the driveway at the front entrance.

The passenger door opens, and I watch a dog jump out, a Chocolate Lab. Her fur is the colour of milk chocolate with just a hint of cinnamon; her pinkish brown nose quivers at the air. Beauty! Can it be? All Chocolate Labs look like that; still, Kyle, her new owner, does go to this school. I see the thick black harness and feel pride rise inside me like the sun. My smile stretches wider. Beauty, my dog (at least my former dog) is performing exactly the way she's supposed to. Tall and mysteriously dark and cool, Kyle grips Beauty's harness.

My heart swells suddenly, an instant ache pulses from my chest. Darn, this can't be happening to me again. No. It's seeing Beauty again, it has to be. I mean, she was my dog for a whole year.

"Hey, he's wearing the same thing as you—your psychic twin."

Alicia's right. Kyle's wearing beige cargoes and a dark green tee shirt. He's even layered the dark green over a beige top.

Why didn't you call, I want to yell at him. Kyle reaches his fingers through his gelled black spikes, his eyes looking up and reflecting the aching blueness of the sky. Will he turn? Will he look my way?

I smile, toss my hair back, and straighten my shoulders.

"Whatever you're doing, you can stop," Alicia snipes at me. "You know he can't see you."

Chapter 2

Kyle and Beauty

It's the first day of school. I stand up from the breakfast table, bend over and touch my shoes to make sure. Left shoe feels fuzzy, and so does the right one. Beige suede loafers—at least that's what I hope both of them are. "Do my shoes match?"

"Uh huh," my sister Shawna answers, her voice directly across from me.

"Your pants are the same colour. Your shirt's beige, too. You look bland. Let me get your green shirt to throw over." A few seconds later, she puts it in my hands.

"Bland, huh. And this green goes with beige, right?" I pull it over my head. It's getting harder for me to remember what colours look like, let alone remember what goes together.

"Yup." Her voice drifts away. She must be leaving the room.

"So, I'll be off then," I tell Dad as I head for the hall too. "Running behind."

"Ah'll give you a lift. Just so happens ah'm goin' right by your school this mornin'."

My father knows I can get to school by myself but he must have promised Mom he'd drive me. She's in bed with the flu. So he uses his southern drawl, stretching out every syllable, making me want to punch a wall in irritation.

"I need to do it myself."

I repeat this line to my family all the time, but today I sound and feel more irritated than I should. First-day-back-to-school nerves. Since I lost my sight, I'm even less confident than before.

"Now, let me see if I have this right...you're runnin' late..."

Bonk, in the background a ball bounces, followed by scrambling, scratching paws and claws, my Chocolate Lab. *Thunk*, the ball landing in my dog's mouth. Shawna is throwing the tennis ball for Beauty, technically okay, since the dog isn't in harness and working, but annoying because Beauty seems to like my sister better than me. And there's that bouncing noise.

Dad ignores it and continues, "...yet you will not accept a lift from me because you wish to establish your independence."

Dad sounds the way his coffee smells—rich, deep, and mellow. A coffee-drip drawl coupled with a Mensa vocabulary; that's my father, the lawyer.

"Would it not be a better idea to establish your independence on a day when, say, you were not at least fifteen minutes," I can hear him tapping his watch crystal here, "behind schedu-el?"

"I wouldn't be late, if you could talk faster." I walk out of the kitchen down the hall to the hat tree.

"...and if Shawna would stop fooling around with Beauty. Beauty, come on now." I grab her harness from a hook and shake it. Then I bend over, hold it out for her, and smile. "Good dog."

The trainer at Canine Vision told us that if the dog doesn't step into the harness immediately, it means there is something wrong. The dog may be sick, or too old and tired. But I worry about something else. What if Beauty just plain realizes I'm not a dog person at all? I used to be really scared of them. Does she sense that I'm relieved when she just comes to me when I call her—especially when my puppy-crazy sister is around?

She pushes her head through the front loop, and, feeling the tug, I pat her head and rub her warm silky ears. She's the only dog that I can rely on. My irritation dissolves. I know I can get to school today without riding in Dad's massive SUV. I can live my life the way I want. I don't have to be afraid. People won't stare at me because of a white cane. They'll stare at this incredible dog, whom Shawna says is beautiful. They won't avoid me for my disability—they'll approach me because I have Beauty. With this confidence, I give in.

"Fine," I say. "The defense rests. Can we go now?"

"One sec," Shawna calls. I feel her hands patting down the flaps on my pants pockets. Then she tugs at my collar and picks something off my shoulder.

"Lint," she tells me.

"Enough!" I grab my backpack from the same hat tree where I hang Beauty's harness.

"All set?" Dad asks. "Shawna, you coming too?"

"No, I'm walking with friends."

Dad doesn't argue with her. Beauty and I walk outside together.

"Car, Beauty," I tell her, and when she stops, I feel for the door handle, lift it, and pull.

"In, girl." We both squeeze into the front together with Beauty on the floor. It's awkward till Beauty turns around and settles, and I arrange my feet around her. I don't want to sit in the back, and I like her close by me.

We drive off with bagpipes playing, Dad's favourite Highland CD. The air-conditioning is going full blast, which is probably just as well since I'm starting to sweat. I breathe in the new-car smell of glue, vinyl, and other carcinogens. Mom loves that scent—she sells cars, and she got the Status with her family discount.

At the third block, Dad turns down the volume on his CD player so he can talk.

"First day of your senior year. It's exciting." Dad sounds more northern the further we get from home. "Can we try for a little less partying? I know the temptation's there, the big last hurrah. But you've got to get those grades up for college, after all."

"Oh, I'm going to work harder, Dad. I promise. What kind of average do you think I need to get into Queens?" Queens is the university Dad went to.

"I think they're askin' for nineties now. But there's a good school not half an hour away from here, son. You don't need to go to Queen's."

"But I want to. It's tradition, right?"

"Sure, son." He pats my shoulder. "We're arriving at your school now. I'll take you in the front driveway. There are four steps up to the front door. You gonna be all right?"

"Yep. Just stop the car." I turn towards him when the car comes to a halt. "I am going to get into Queens, Dad. I know you don't think so, but I will."

"I believe you can do anything you set your mind to, Kyle." He pauses for a moment, his southern breather. "But don't always make things hard for yourself. Life's given you enough challenges."

I shrug him off. "See ya, Dad." Beauty and I climb out.

Freedom. I inhale deeply. Even though it's hot today, I can smell the fall coming. It's a spicy, almost smoky scent that hangs over the warmth. In another few weeks, the air will bite and leaves will change colours—the second fall that

I won't be able to watch it happen. To me, red and orange have changed into tastes, like apples and tangerines.

"Find the stairs, Beauty." I hear her whine.

"What's up, girl?" It's as if she's spotted something that's upset her. She finally moves forward and stops at the first stair. I count the three steps and Beauty pauses at the landing, waiting for my instructions. It's working. I'm all by myself, and I'm heading into the school. Once we step inside, the air is thick with smells: salami, sneakers, cherry bubble gum, sweat, floral deodorant, all mixed together.

I'd hoped to be earlier, so the halls wouldn't be crowded. Kids jostle past me. And it doesn't seem to faze Beauty at all.

"Hello, Doggie." "Hi, Puppy." Beauty gets about four hellos to my one. We take the stairs and I run my hand along the wall, and then along the metal lockers till I get to mine.

"Yo, Kyle, my man. What's happenin'?" It's Ryan, who talks a little different when he's nervous—ghetto-speak, like a rapper. My dad has wondered out loud whether Ryan's wearing his father's pants, and whether his belt succeeds in holding them up, since the crotch hangs down by his ankles. Guess he dresses the part of a rapper, too.

"I like the dog," Ryan tells me. "This is a new angle we'll have to explore. Dogs are chick magnets."

"I believe you're right," I answer, although, how would Ryan know? He hasn't been the least bit lucky with the female half of the population. "We should probably get you a mutt."

I hang up my bag in the locker, taking my new digital recorder out and slipping it into my pocket. Then Beauty and I walk ahead of Ryan, back to the stairs towards our first class. She stops at the top of the stairs. I reach my foot out to touch the edge of the step. Beauty whines softly, just like she did outside the school.

And then I hear a voice: high and musical, like chimes in a wind. It's Elizabeth, the girl who raised Beauty.

"Beauty!" she calls, and before I can give a command, the dog bolts down the stairs.

One hand on the railing, the other still gripping the harness, I stumble after Beauty. I can't even count the steps, I'm going down so fast. Any second I will pitch over, and my face will scrape down the edges of the remaining stairs.

"No, Beauty!" I yank at her leash to give her a correction. She finally stops, at the bottom, like she's supposed to.

"Man, you all right?" Ryan asks me, his voice coming up from behind me.

"What is with that chick? Is she nuts? Calling your dog's name, then running away."

I shake out my hand, which feels burnt from its speed ride down the railing. "Did she have red hair?"

"Uh huh. Hot but a little young." Ryan thumps my back. "You don't want to mess with her. She's out of your league. It said so right on her shirt."

CHAPTER 3

Elizabeth and Magic

Standing in front of her locker mirror, Alicia is untacking, re-twisting, and re-tacking her hair back on top of her head. "Phew, wish we had air conditioning in this place." She fans at herself with one hand.

"Why didn't you tell me?" I accuse her, as I tackle my combination lock.

"Tell you what?" Alicia asks.

I point to the words emblazoned on my shirt. OUT OF YOUR LEAGUE. But Alicia peels off her sweater at that moment, and across the front of her tank top in sparkly gold letters is the word HOT.

"Never mind." I shake my head wearily as I throw my junk in the locker.

"Meet you in class. I gotta use the can." I snap my lock shut again and duck into the washroom to attack the stain on my own top. The wet blob that forms around my chest has grown even larger. I lean forward for a better look, and the wet sink counter leaves a horizontal mark across my crotch.

"Perfect, perfect," I mutter at my mirror image.

I turn Alicia's top inside out and reach to the back of my neck to rip the label away. The fuzzy seams run down my shoulder and around my armpit, standing up in a small ridge. My shirt looks just the way I feel—all inside out.

Poor Kyle—he nearly performed a head-first slide down the stairs. I shouldn't have called out Beauty's name like that. I suck in my cheeks and brush on more shading under the bones, another layer of mascara over already crusty lashes. Best I can do. Can't delay facing the rest of high school any longer. I sigh and dash out again, down the long empty corridor.

My first class is English, and I hesitate outside the open door. Five minutes late and the packed classroom already sits in a death-watch kind of silence. Another breath, then I bustle in, wincing at the teacher, hoping she won't ask for a late slip. She smiles at me as I slide into a seat behind Alicia.

Mrs. Dejean talks about the wonderful adventure we're going to have with Shakespeare this term. She's a tiny woman with bright eyes and a big voice, and she belts out some of Willy Boy's most famous lines: "To be or not to be..." "A rose by any other name..." Then she launches into a love sonnet, which sounds pretty enough, but does anyone really understand a word? Mrs. Dejean holds her hand to her heart and recites as though she is in love, "My mistress' eyes are nothing like the sun."

Instantly, I think of Kyle's eyes. They're nothing like the sun either—more like the sky, expansive, blue.

Willy-Boy talks about all the colours his love is not; her lips aren't coral red, and her breasts aren't snow white. (The guys at the back of the class chuckle at the word breasts. Idiots. The hats they're wearing on their heads in this heat must be roasting their brains.) Willy's girl doesn't smell great or sound like music.

And yet, by heaven, I think my love as rare
As any she belied with false compare.

Even though he keeps telling us what she isn't, I get the feeling his love for her makes all her colours and smells a thousand times better.

I look down at my pants and notice that the juice stain at my knee shows again ever so faintly. I roll my eyes. I wish love would make this berry colour fade. Love? I try to shake myself out of it. Whose love am I thinking about? All that fills my head is an image of Kyle, tripping down the stairs, which is ridiculous because clearly he can't see colours, nor are we in love with each other. But I shouldn't have run away from him. I should have stopped, made sure he was all right and apologized for calling Beauty. Too late now—stupid stupid.

I still have French to sit through before lunch period.

The to-be verb, *être: Je suis, tu es, il/elle/on est, nous sommes, vous êtes, ils/elles sont.* My mind wanders, coming back to back with Willy's "To be or not to be" (English is by far my more favourite subject), I find myself confusing the lines, trying to translate them in my mind—*Etre ou pas être*, not quite as musical. We do *passé composé* and finally future: *je serai, tu seras, il sera*. Hey, I know a saying with that verb in it: "*Qué sera sera*." What will be will be—is that French or Shakespeare? Or both? Maybe Shakespeare wrote in French or got translated.

I wonder about that line. Do we have to accept things 'being' and 'happening' randomly? Do we just sit around and wait?

I don't think so.

So I decide right then. I am going back to the senior floor to try to talk to Kyle. First, I'll apologize, then we'll take it from there. Just talking to the guy isn't breaking my deal with Alicia. Not when she's wearing Boy Catcher cologne.

The bell buzzes, and I'm off, down the hall. Senior lunch is at 1:00, so I head upstairs to the top floor to look for Kyle, against a tide of kids coming down.

Bump, bump. "Excuse me." "Sorry."

I feel all bruised when I finally make it. Then I kind of sneak around, ducking behind people till I spot him outside the chemistry lab. He can't see me so he'll never know I'm there unless I speak to him.

I walk closer, watching how he touches Beauty's head ever

so gently. That gives me time to get up my nerve. I take another half step and stop. If I go closer now, I'll disturb them. Beauty will break for me. I know it. I can't do it!

Now I've lost my nerve, so I decide to walk right by. They've formed the perfect bond between dog guide and human. If Kyle is good to Beauty, that's what matters most. He loves Beauty; he doesn't have to like me.

If it hadn't been for Beauty, I could have made it past without him ever knowing. But she sees me and barks. It's a curious mix between a roar of joy and a howl of pain, not her regular bark at all. I walk faster, hoping she'll behave the way she's been trained, but she's bucking like a horse that's trying to throw its rider.

I duck down the next stairwell feeling that life is so unfair. I can't even go near Kyle without distracting Beauty from her most important purpose. Never mind, I tell myself. Alicia and I made a pact—a solo year, no boys to mess us up. What difference does it make if Beauty can't function as a dog guide with me around? I'm going to leave Kyle alone anyway, for my own sake as well as his and Beauty's.

At home, after school, lying back in the comfort of my unmade bed, I wonder about fostering another dog for Canine Vision. Will it be better when I have my own dog again—a whole year of another Beauty?

"All set?" Mom calls as she bustles in the door.

She pokes her head into my room and wrinkles her nose

at the mess. "Did you know you have your shirt on inside out? Better change that."

I think about telling her that I like it that way, just so she doesn't get her way all the time. But I'm anxious to switch, myself. I grab one of Debra's black hand-me-down tops. That should go with beige, too. When I slip it on, ready to pick up my new dog, I feel right-side-out again. Mom honks the horn so I hustle out the door.

"Eww." I pick up a baby bottle full of what looks like cottage cheese off the floor of the van.

"Never mind now. Hop in."

"Fine." I sweep the baby junk off the seat. The van smells of sour milk, and Mom keeps her window rolled down as we drive off to Canine Vision.

"Air conditioning's bad for the environment anyway," she tells me when I complain about the heat. It's a long drive but at least traffic's good and we get there quickly.

All around the brick building, we can see trainers and volunteers walking dogs, some in harness and others with leashes and jackets. I notice a wiry Border terrier wearing an orange jacket—a hearing-ear dog—and think how wild it would be to try to train one of those.

Mom parks in the back, and the moment we step in the building I smell the earthy, sock smell of dog. I realize how much I've missed that smell since Beauty left. I grin, walking a little quicker. Mom really moves to keep up as we head to the puppy program office. It's a small room, covered with framed photographs of blind owners and their dog guides—same grey speckled linoleum floor as the hall, shaded with clumps of dog hair. Natalie, a dark-haired lady who loves dogs as much as I do, smiles as she gets up from behind her desk.

"Ready to meet Magic?" she asks.

I smack my forehead with my hand. "That's the dog's name. I wondered why Mom called her 'magic'."

"We're hoping she will be." Natalie winks at me. "I'll go get her."

Mom and I sit on the wooden armchairs against the wall opposite Natalie's desk. My grin grows wider, even as the chair grows harder beneath my butt. A new puppy—I love everything about them: floppy ears and paws, roly-poly bodies and rabbit-soft fur. They smell like hamburger, and they bounce around you to play. You can't be unhappy around a puppy.

The door opens, and in walks a grownup-looking Golden Retriever. Is this the surprise Mom mentioned? Her eyes are golden brown, and she shows just enough white around them to let us know that she feels worried about the whole situation. She stops and looks at me for a moment. She must decide I'm okay. Her body changes mood almost instantly. Her tail wags, and the long golden hair from it sweeps the floor.

"How old is Magic?"

"Ten months," Natalie answers.

Magic walks over to me, and I pat my teenaged dog.

"But that means we'll only have her for a little while," I protest.

Magic licks my hand fervently, as though desperate to make up for the time we've lost together.

"I'm sorry. It's just you're so experienced, and Magic's other family had to move to England on short notice. The big bonus is that Magic's toilet trained and well-behaved. She's already had a great assessment."

"She's supposed to be wonderful with kids," Mom said.

"Definitely—the previous family had a five-year-old and a three-year-old. Plus there's one more consideration."

"What do you mean?" I ask.

"Magic is a purebred Golden Retriever, and we have her papers—which means we're considering her for the breeding program."

"That means we'll be able to keep her?"

"Well, if her eyes, elbows, and hips check out. We'd only bring her in to breed, and then whelp and nurse her puppies."

"Mom?" I look at her and she nods and smiles.

I slip off the chair and kneel down on the floor throwing my arms around my new dog.

"Magic," I whisper and lean my head on top of hers.

"Don't look so worried. We're going to be together a long, long time."

"While Magic is coming along really well, she does seem a

bit disoriented by the move from her original family. Just have patience with her." Natalie smiles at us.

Magic turns to me and laps at my face. I squeeze my eyes and mouth closed tight to protect against drool.

"Well, we know you will be, or we wouldn't ask you to take her."

My own permanent dog—I sigh and stand up, ready to take Magic home. Back out the door, I walk her a bit, and once we're on the grass, I tell her, "Do your business." She looks at me again with the whites of her eyes showing.

"Well, if you don't have to go, suit yourself. But you'll be stuck in the car a while."

We get back in the van, and Magic actually leaps into Teal's car seat, bumping her head on the ceiling.

"Uh, uh, you're not the baby," I tell her and tug the leash so that she comes in the front and sits on the floor at my feet. She sniffs at Teal's bottle of congealed milk and settles around it. As we drive, I pick long golden hairs from my black shirt. I love having dog hair back in my life.

Magic opens her mouth and pants heavily. She whines softly after a while.

"It's okay girl. It'll be all right. You're with us and you'll never change owners again."

"Careful," Mom says. "You can't count on that. You know that large dogs can have hip problems."

"But that's okay, too. Don't you see? If she flunks on

health, we can adopt her. One way or the other we'll always have Magic."

Life's too perfect, I think. We're driving by the park now, and outside I see Kyle strolling along. What are the odds? Magic senses another dog and stands up, paws on my knees for a moment, till she jumps onto my lap.

Kyle's walking Beauty, and of course he can't see us. But Beauty can. She turns to look at the van and freezes. She looks at the dog in my lap and then looks towards me, not moving. Kyle reaches his hand in front of his head like he's feeling for an obstacle.

Beauty's golden eyes don't accuse, they accept and love, but they don't understand.

"Down, Magic." I gently force my new permanent dog back down onto the floor. I duck down too. I can't face the hurt in Beauty's eyes.

Chapter 4

Kyle and Beauty

For some reason our English class is held in the chemistry lab, which smells like some kind of strong medicine. Not too many kids into the sciences, I guess. I hate sitting on a high stool, so far away from Beauty. I feel out of balance. When I lean over the counter, I accidentally slip into what turns out to be a sink. Beauty barks a sharp announcement.

"Are you all right, Kyle?" It's my ex-girlfriend's voice.

"Maddie, hi—I'm fine."

I quickly push myself up and straighten on the stool again. I can feel Beauty's nose sniffing at me. She must be standing.

"Settle, girl. I'm all right. How are you?" I ask Maddie, in the tone I wish she had used for me, one friend to another, rather than one friend worried about the other.

"Good." A long, awkward pause—I miss being able to

see whether a person is waiting for a response from me. Maybe she's already turned away and talking to someone on her right. No, she starts talking to me again.

"I heard we get to choose our own novels this year. What a relief. No more *Lord of the Flies* or *A Separate Peace*."

"Maybe something from this decade," I agree with her. I remember Maddie and I hated *A Separate Peace* together, my fondest memory of English class.

I sense when the teacher comes into the room. The atmosphere changes but the conversations continue.

"It's old man Veen. He's the toughest English teacher in the school. Darn, I thought he was supposed to retire last year," Maddie whispers at me.

"He's flashing the lights to get our attention."

I smile.

"Won't work on me." It doesn't work on anyone else either because the talking continues. Suddenly, a door slams, violently. Maddie gasps.

"Thank you for your attention." Chalk screeches and pounds along the blackboard.

"My name is Mr.Veen." His voice sounds dry and hard. "A laboratory for English class is ridiculous and unacceptable. I will have this changed for tomorrow."

He calls out our names for attendance. By the change in the volume in his voice, I sense him drawing nearer.

"Kyle Nicholson," he calls.

"Present," I answer.

"A dog in my class. Perhaps somebody will learn something this term." Dry, hard, and sarcastic.

"Beauty is my dog guide."

"How do you get your reading done, Kyle? Do you have an Educational Assistant?"

"Not for English, sir. I scan the work into my computer, and it reads it to me. Or I get the book on CD."

"I don't see why the board can't assign an assistant to you. Am I supposed to prepare a less accelerated program for you?" he asks.

"No, sir! I'll do the full workload, like everyone else."

"I'll hold you to that, Kyle." A challenge or a warning—Veen doesn't sound convinced. But I'll show him and Dad at the same time. I may be blind, but I can work twice as hard as everyone else and still get into any university.

When Veen is finished taking attendance, he talks about his expectations for the term. He calls us up to choose a book for independent study from the box at the front of the room.

I'm not about to muscle my way through the other kids to get first choice. So I hang back and wait.

"Mr. Nicholson, do you need a special invitation?" Veen asks.

"Forward, Beauty," I say, but before I make it to the box, Maddie puts a book in my hands.

"I can do it myself," I hiss at her.

"But it's the last one. *Lord of the Flies*."

"Aw geeze," I grumble. "Mr. Veen, I read this book in grade nine, and I read it again in grade ten."

"It's a wonderful book, isn't it? Stands the test of time—addresses real issues."

"For sure. But there must be other books that are just as good."

I don't mean it sarcastically, but some of the kids titter, which gets Veen angry.

"You'll read *Lord of the Flies*."

"Sir. What if I go to the library and get several books on CD, and you select one from those?"

"That would be special treatment. I thought we already agreed there would be no alternate program for you."

The class turns quiet. Everyone's enjoying the show-down, waiting and wondering if I'll snap back at him. I'm determined not to turn this into a high-noon gunfight. What student ever wins one of those, anyway?

"Studying the same book three times is a little much, even in a regular program."

"All right."

Like the old gunslinger of the classroom, Veen takes his time before firing his last bullet.

"You've read the assigned novel twice. So, find another book and compare and contrast it with *Lord of the Flies* in your essay."

Compare and contrast, two deadly words, double the work and doubly dull. But I don't want to argue anymore, or go back on my position. I want to prove to him and everyone else that I can make it on my own.

"Yes sir." I decide right then that English will be my least favourite subject this year.

For the rest of the class, Veen discusses essay format, introductory paragraph, line of argument, and supporting fact. Then he gives out an assignment sheet that warns: *No abridged versions of these novels are acceptable.*

"Do you want some help to your next class, Kyle?" Maddie asks when the bell goes.

"No, thanks. I have Beauty. She's got to do the job."

"You replaced me with a dog?" Maddie is only half-joking.

"I'll never replace you."

Maddie was the first love of my life, as far back as kindergarten. I can't remember anymore quite what she looked like, but the vibes she gives off are like sunshine and oranges—warm, bright with a scent of tangy sweetness. She couldn't handle me going blind, and I couldn't handle what we had become: the helper and helpless.

She touches my hand.

"Bye, Kye." I think I hear a smile in her voice.

"Forward, girl. Find the door." The moment we step into the hall, Beauty freezes.

"What's wrong, Beauty?"

It's not like her. I reach my arm ahead and feel above for obstacles. She'd stop if there were a dangling branch or

wire. She's done that before. Nothing. I stretch my leg out as far as it will go and touch my foot down. No hole there. No obstruction either. I inhale deeply, and I smell baby powder or lotion—and put that scent and Beauty's behaviour together. Beauty barks now, *Rawf, rawf, rawf, rawf!*

She pulls upwards. Is she standing on her hind legs?

"No!" I shake her harness.

"Beauty, you can't fall apart every time you see Elizabeth." I run my fingers through my hair, feeling a little unhinged myself.

"Hey man, I got French next. What about you?" another voice barks beside me.

"Quick, Ryan. Look around. Is she here?"

"Who, where?" He pauses, as he must see whom I mean.

"Forget her, dude. She's too young for you." There's disdain in his voice, but Ryan isn't normally so discerning. Breathing and being female are his only usual qualifications. He's trying to put me off her because he thinks I haven't got a chance.

"So she was here. I knew it. I smelled her."

"Great, sharp nose there. A little red-haired girl was checking out the dog. That's all. She didn't even look your way."

"What do you know?"

"Hey, man, we don't have to argue this one out. There's one simple way to find out. Call her."

"I don't have her number."

I hear Ryan sigh. "Have you ever heard of 'Information'? Just dial them up, and they'll get her number for you. Heck, I bet they'll even dial it for you if you tell them you're handicapped."

"I'm not handicapped. I'm blind."

"My grandmother's not handicapped either. She makes the phone company dial for her all the time 'cause she's lazy."

Ryan is amazing in both his level of immaturity and his sudden pure insights. I could call the operator and make her do the work for me. I don't need to involve my sister Shawna at all—the big road block to most of my personal calls.

Algebra and geometry are scheduled for the afternoon, and for those classes an Educational Assistant does help me. The EA smells like old coffee and sounds slightly squeaky when she tells me the equations. I try to picture the numbers and letters in my head, but it's exhausting. Plus, she pats my back when I do get the right answer. I think I prefer tough guy Veen's approach. Still, in between the exponents and brackets, another picture keeps drifting into my head, which makes me feel a lot better. I see myself calling the operator after school. My reward for all this will be to speak to Elizabeth. It's been on my mind all August, but today I will make it happen.

At the end of the day, Beauty and I leave through the front door of the school, turning left at the sidewalk for about twenty steps to the bus shelter. We practised this a few times last week. I could just say, "Bus stop," and she'd lead me there, but I count my steps instead because I don't want to become too dependent.

There's a warm wind blowing, which makes the glass panels in the bus shelter creak. I hope we're not in for a thunderstorm—I'll get drenched.

"Can I give him my bologna sandwich?" a young voice interrupts my thoughts.

"No, sorry. She's working right now; she's not allowed to accept food."

"Guess I'll just throw it in the garbage then." Clunk. "She's a cool dog. What's her name?"

I mumble an answer because I'm too tired to make conversation. A bus swishes to the side of us, puffing out diesel fumes as it pulls in the curb. I shuffle forward with Beauty. We climb the stairs, and I reach out for the box to put my token.

"It's over here," the little boy's voice says as he pushes my hand closer.

I shouldn't feel irritated because I know he's trying to help. He can't possibly know what it's like to be pushed by somebody you don't know. I keep my cool, and I ask him whether the front seat is empty.

"Uh huh," he answers, and he squeezes by us. "Here, girl," he calls from close by.

"She's supposed to do it herself," I say.

"Find the seat, Beauty," I command and then I slide in beside the kid.

The bus lurches ahead, stops for a second and then jerks forward again. I grab for Beauty.

"She can sit on top of my feet. I don't mind. I'm going to get my own dog some day, a dog just like her. Can I pat her?"

I drop the harness, keeping the leash tucked under my own feet. Beauty doesn't like the bus much and always finds it hard to settle.

"Sorry, the rules are that I have to take the harness off for anyone else to touch or talk to her, and that would take too long."

Donald–that's what his name is–wants to know all about Beauty and all about me.

"How did you go blind?"

"Retinopathy," I tell him flatly, hoping the big word will scare him off the topic. Sometimes I like to escape this area of conversation that seems to dominate my life. But clearly it isn't going to be today.

"What's that?" he continues.

I sigh. A bright kid–save me from a bright kid's questions. Still, I always feel I have to answer them.

"Well, I have diabetes which sometimes causes the blood vessels in a person's eyes to bleed."

"My grandfather has diabetes, and he doesn't even wear glasses except to read."

"Your grandfather probably has Type 2, which means he got it when he was older. He can probably control it with the right diet. I have the other kind. I've had it for quite a while, and when you don't control your blood sugar levels really well, complications can arise."

"You mean you didn't control your blood sugar, and you went blind? That sucks."

"Yeah, it does."

Something we both can agree on. Still, now we're at the point I hate, the inevitable moment of pity, when a sighted person almost flat out tells you that they'd rather be dead than blind. I can hear it in Donald's voice. The moment is here.

"But you have this way-cool, super-smart dog. You are sooo lucky."

"Lucky?" I smile as I pat Beauty. Yeah, Donald's right. Today I feel lucky, and I'll feel even luckier when I get to speak to Elizabeth again.

CHAPTER 5

Elizabeth and Magic

It's raining hard as the van rolls into the driveway, and we make a run for the house the moment Mom pulls the key from the ignition. Magic bolts for the door alongside me, and the first thing she does once she's inside is squat on the carpet.

"You're supposed to be toilet-trained!" I yank her hard and manage to drag her outside to finish her pee. The drizzle plasters her golden fur back, and she gives me a critical look as though I should make it stop.

"Business, Magic. Do all your business. We're not going in until you do."

A sliver of anxious white rims her golden eyes as she looks from me to the washed-out grey sky. She shakes herself. It's final. There will be no more business right now, and we're both getting drenched.

"Okay, if you're sure you don't have to go." I lead

Magic back inside. "Let me show you your crate." We head to the kitchen and, there, shock of shock, sits Rolph, my sister's ex-boyfriend. What's he doing here? I wonder.

I always thought he looked suspiciously corporate for an animations guy. He's got a thick body, blond bushy hair, a sharp nose, and controlling grey eyes. He's crouched down, holding his arms out to his son, who's manoeuvring around the table.

"Come on Teal, you can do it."

"He's eight months old. Give it up, he's not going to walk," I tell Rolph, as Magic and I come into the room.

At the sight of the dog, Teal's face brightens with glee, and he staggers towards Magic, holding out a baby cookie. Magic pads up, sniffs the cookie, then starts licking Teal's face, getting giggles that transform into squeals.

"Here, stop that." Rolph pushes Magic away.

Teal holds out his cookie again, which Magic bites, then Teal stuffs the crumbs in his mouth.

"The dog took his food. Elizabeth, surely that isn't right." Rolph stands up.

Magic's lip raises, and she growls, soft and low.

Rolph backs away. "This dog is aggressive, Elizabeth!"

"She's just trying to protect Teal," I protest. Already, Magic doesn't like Rolph, which I can fully understand.

"Magic! Go lie down!" I point to the crate, a large cage we keep for our foster dogs. It's not supposed to be a punishment, more like the dog's own personal bedroom, a safe haven from people like Rolph.

Magic gives Teal's face another wash with her tongue, and then pads quietly into the crate. She lies down on the blanket and crosses her front legs, dropping her jaw into a relaxed dog grin. It's clear she's happy and comfortable knowing there's a toddler in the house.

"Rolph, I didn't know you were here." My mother walks in, changed from her work clothes into a brown tracksuit with GO FOR IT across the top. She rubs a towel over her damp hair.

"Hello, Sarah. I gave Deb the use of my apartment so that she would have a quiet space to work. When it was time to pick up Teal from daycare, it seemed only fair that I take a turn, since she's on a deadline."

"Your job not working out?" Mom continues as she takes some red peppers from the fridge.

"I'm working freelance these days." Rolph quickly changes the subject. "Really, this new foster dog of yours seems dangerous. Not the kind of dog we want around Teal at all."

"She's not our standard foster dog either." I grin at Rolph. "We're going to keep her."

I glance back at Magic as I reach into the cupboard for a snack. Paws still crossed, head on top of them now—but her floppy ears lift slightly at the rattle of the cookie bag. I turn back towards Rolph.

"Maybe she shouldn't have growled at you, but it's Magic's first day here. Cut her some slack."

"Well, if you put a dog's life ahead of a child's, maybe Teal will have to live elsewhere."

Mom and I give each other looks. There's the threat. It's always there. Our family worries Rolph will go to court for joint custody. So we all act nice through gritted teeth whenever he's around. Rolph scoops up Teal and plants slurpy kisses on his face. What's really different about what he and Magic do to Teal? A dog's mouth is clean; Rolph's mouth is like an ashtray.

Mom slams a cleaver through a red pepper.

"Magic is wonderful with children, according to the trainers," Mom says brusquely. "Today, as Elizabeth said, we really have to make allowances."

"As long as you watch Teal around her, I guess it should be fine."

"Did you want to stay for supper, Rolph?" My mother raises her cleaver towards him. Why does she have to ask him to stay?

"If you don't mind looking after Teal, I'll order some takeout food for Deb and me. That way she can keep working if she likes."

I can see Mom do a mini eye roll. She doesn't like getting stuck with Teal any more than I do. I watch her open her mouth to say no, but then she shuts it again, shaking her head.

"Tell Deb she shouldn't stay out late. I can't be up with Teal tonight and teach class tomorrow."

Phew, safe. No Rolph at dinner time.

Rolph gets up to leave and then says over his shoulder, "By the way, someone called for you."

"Who?"

"A boy." Rolph taps his chin with a finger.

"Well, that narrows it down," I say through gritted teeth. I feel the blood rush to my face because I want it to be Kyle so badly.

"You don't remember his name?"

He shakes his head. "Clint, no, Carl...I'm sorry, I was chasing Teal, and I didn't have time to write it down. But you can listen to the voice mail yourself, anyway."

"Kyle?" I venture.

Rolph snaps his fingers. "That's it. He said something about Rollerblading. You made a date with him in the summer. He left several messages—you can listen to them all. They didn't make any sense to me."

I run to the phone, key in our private voice mail code—a code Rolph's somehow gotten hold of—and hear Kyle's voice: "Hi, Elizabeth, I don't know if you remember me, but you told me at Beauty's graduation that you'd show me how to Rollerblade some time. Call me back." Beep!

Next message. "Kyle again—forgot to leave you my telephone number: 336-9401."

Does he just want to Rollerblade with someone, or does he want to see me, I wonder. The next message plays.

"Hi; it's Kyle Nicholson again. If you don't want to Rollerblade, call me anyway, we can do something else."

Fourth and final message: "Well, I guess you're still not home. I just wanted to talk. You took off so quickly at school today...maybe you just want to forget it. I'll understand. Oh yeah, it's Kyle calling."

He sounds nervous. I smile. The first few times I met Kyle, he seemed so ultra cool and unreachable. "Dude with an attitude"—that's what Alicia called him. Now here he is calling me, and he's nervous! Whoo-hoo! I listen to the messages again to get his number. I take some deep breaths to calm myself as I think of what to say. *I'd love to show you how to Rollerblade*. Nah, too desperate. *If you'd like to go Rollerblading, I can show you*. I start keying in his number: Three, three, six. The square buttons feel slippery under my fingers. Whoops, was that a nine I pressed? Four, zero, one—wait. A man's voice answers. Voice mail. He speaks in a Southern accent. Darn! I've dialed the wrong number. I slam the phone down before I get to the message part.

I wash my hands and dry my fingers carefully. Then I go again: three, three, six, nine, four, zero, one. No finger slipping; for sure it has to be his number—again the Southern accent. I listen through the entire message this time and leave my own. It all comes out in a rush.

"If you wanna go Rollerblading, meet me at the swings in the park at 5:00 Friday."

CHAPTER 6

Kyle and Beauty

Why hasn't Elizabeth returned my calls? I made enough of them. Perhaps that's the problem: I sounded too desperate. Why would she want to go out with a blind guy anyway?

To take my mind off Elizabeth, I decide to work on my school project for Mr. Veen. I've gone on the Internet to search for audio books that might satisfy him. The special program on my computer reads my screen to me. I've put the voice on high speed, but it's still too slow. I stop when I hear the word Blindness. It's a Nobel Prize-winning novel by José Saramago. How can Mr. Veen argue with that?

I hear Mom walk in the door and set her bags down in the hall. She sighs when I ask her to drive me to the library.

"Just let me get a cup of tea, will you, Kyle?"

While she's making it, I tell her about my day at school. I leave out the bit about Elizabeth, and the way Beauty seems to act up around her. Instead, I focus on Mr. Veen.

"Sounds as though Mr. Veen has a bit of an attitude problem," says my mother. "Perhaps your father and I should have a word with the principal about him."

Mom always wants to make things right for me.

"No, Mom," I say firmly. "You can't always step in to protect me. All I have to do is prove myself to him, just like everyone else."

"You're right," Mom says, making a clatter with her teacup as she sets it down. "The best revenge is living well."

"Which means?"

"Your essay has to knock his socks off. Come on. The library closes in an hour. Let's go."

I harness up Beauty again, and we head off to the car. Outside it smells like wet sidewalk—it must have rained. I can't see it, but I feel the warm lightness of the sun on my face. As I pull open the car door, I hear the ringing, insistent and unmistakable, of the phone.

I squeeze my eyelids together. It's Elizabeth, I know it's her.

"We're in a hurry. Let's just let the answering machine get it," Mom says.

No, no, I need to hear her voice. But Mom's slammed her door already, the engine's starting up.

With a heavy feeling in my chest, I slide in too. We don't talk as we drive to the library. Mom's mind is probably back at work. I'm wondering what's on Elizabeth's phone message.

When we get to the parking lot, Mom offers me her arm.

"You can drop the harness. It will be faster."

"No, thanks. Forward, girl." I love being able to do this myself and actually walk ahead of Mom.

"Find the door, Beauty."

When we step into the library, I inhale the earthy book smell, the paper and glue. The floor feels almost smooth beneath my feet, a low pile carpet, but as we move forward, Beauty pulls to the left, as if she's distracted by something or somebody. I shake her harness as a correction just as a female voice tells me that dogs are not allowed in the library. A young voice—probably a library page.

"It is illegal for you to prevent a dog guide from a public building," my mother tells her in a sharp, hard tone.

This is just the kind of attention I don't want to have. Explaining gently that Beauty is a dog guide would have probably solved the problem. I smile into thin air, hoping the page understands I'm just with my mother for the ride—that we don't share the same attitude. But I can't give Beauty directions to the audio department, so

I'm forced to drop the harness and take Mom's arm.

"Beauty seems to like that girl. She keeps turning her head to look at her," Mom tells me.

"No, Beauty, no!" I say loudly and shake the harness.

"Maybe you should call the trainer about that."

"Let me handle the dog, Mom."

I wonder if the page has red hair. What would Mom say if she knew how Beauty had bolted down the stairs after Elizabeth?

While Mom and I peruse the audio shelves together, Beauty stands patiently at my feet, the perfect dog guide. It gets really hot waiting while Mom reads all the titles in the S section. "José Saramago, here it is—*Blindness*," she finally says.

"Can you check if it's unabridged?" I wipe sweat from my forehead with a shaky hand. Suddenly, I feel really sick.

"It doesn't say that anywhere on the cover. *Three hours of reading*. Ah, here—it's a condensed version approved by the author."

"A condensed version won't do. Mr. Veen will only accept a complete book." Standing is becoming an effort, and I shift from one leg to the other. My knees wobble. Beauty whimpers. "Shh, girl."

"You know what? We'll take this one out, and I'll buy you a copy of the book on the way home. You can scan it, or I personally will read it out loud to you. We'll show this guy."

She's pumped from her victory with the library page, and I can hear the determination in her voice. But I feel vague and confused. She works Saturdays and three evenings a week selling cars. We won't be home enough hours together for her to read it out loud to me. And I will be the one calling all the attention to myself in English class with the toughest teacher at our school.

"Mom, can you find me the audio of *Lord of the Flies* too? Under G for Golding. William."

I can feel myself turning grey. My legs and arms turn into Jell-O, quivery and weak.

"Why? You backing down?"

"No, no, Mom. It's a comparative essay. I need both books."

I find and grip Beauty's harness tightly, to steady myself.

"Kyle, you're trembling. What's wrong?"

Beauty whimpers again.

I shake my head and grope my backpack for the small bottle of corn syrup I keep in the outside pocket. *Hurry, hurry*, I tell my fumbling fingers as I unzip it and remove the bottle. Unscrewing the cap, I feel my legs buckling, and I sink to the ground. From behind me, I hear a gasp. I get the cap off and have two swallows.

"Should I call an ambulance?" a hushed voice asks, the same page who wanted to keep Beauty out. Great, more attention that I don't want.

Mom ignores her. Beauty licks at my face.

"Did you have your snack after school, the way you're supposed to?" Mom asks.

The answer is clear, and I'm too weak and disoriented to answer.

"Will he be okay? Should I get him some water?" the worried young voice asks.

"I'm fine," I struggle to get the words out. "Please, just go away."

"For heaven's sakes, we were having tea. You couldn't remember to have an arrowroot biscuit at the same time?" my mother rants.

"Don't you understand how important it is to maintain good control over your blood sugar level?" I can hear her through a haze, exasperation hissing through her voice.

The trembling stops, and I can focus on a clear thought again. How can she think I don't understand? I'm the one blind from diabetes. I'm the one who feels like a leaf shaken from a branch. A tide washes over me as the corn syrup connects. I'm exhausted, but I'm better. I breathe deeply.

"Let's just go."

Back in the car, Mom asks if I still want to stop at the bookstore.

"No. I'm wiped."

"We better get home and get some supper into you then."

We drive in silence. I'm fine now, no shakes and yet none of the tell-tale irritability of hyperglycemia either. Still, I feel low. I want my life in control.

The car rolls into the driveway. Mom slams her door and hurries ahead of me to unlock the door. By the time I make it in, she's already checked the answering machine.

"Kyle, some young girl called for you. She didn't identify herself."

I don't even unhitch the dog but head right for the phone in the kitchen, grabbing the receiver from Mom.

I listen to Elizabeth's voice on the message. Chimes in the wind. She wants to meet me in the park Friday at 5:00. I feel everything inside me lift again. Life is good.

Chapter 7

Elizabeth and Magic

"And you left the ironing board out with the iron plugged in! That's four times this week." Mom jams a cereal bowl into the dishwasher as she rants at me.

Across the table from me, Debra tries to coax Teal into eating but he only natters in his high chair, his cheeks blotchy with red clouds.

I chugalug the last of my orange juice so I can answer Mom.

"I didn't leave the iron out. I just set it up so it would be the right temperature to straighten my hair when I'm done eating."

Suddenly, an angry flip of Teal's hand sends his cereal bowl flying, most of the contents landing on Debra. She jumps up and sweeps the Cheerios onto the floor. The phone rings. Mom's tea kettle whistles. Magic barks. From the bedroom, Dad hollers about not having any more clean socks.

It's surround-sound chaos, as usual.

I snap my fingers at the dog.

"Magic, here! Leave those Cheerios alone! You're not supposed to eat the baby's food."

"Let him, just this once." Debra flings up her hands. "I don't feel like cleaning up. Teal was up all night with his teething."

Debra is pale and her hair looks like she's taken a mixer to it, but it also seems wet and spiky. The messy hedgehog style might be on purpose.

"Rolph doesn't like Magic around Teal when he's eating."

Mom continues clearing the table and loading the dishwasher.

"And we can't have it both ways. Elizabeth, be a good girl and clean up that mess so your sister can change for her appointment."

"Magic, in your crate!" I tell her, and she slinks off instantly. Apart from that one piddle on the carpet, Magic does seem perfectly trained.

Hands on my hips, I study the mess on the floor. Always, always, I have to *be a good girl* because of my sister. The Cheerios sit, swollen and soggy in a puddle of milk. I can't just sweep them. I bend down and scoop them up in my hand, yuck, and dump them in the trash. Then I have to get rags to soak up the milk because Mom doesn't allow paper towels—they're not environmental. The gross wet rags will smell rotten in about five minutes, so Mom suggests I be a good girl again and put them in the washing machine downstairs, with a load of Dad's socks.

I don't feel like being good. But I take a deep breath and head down the stairs to the laundry with a hamper and the milk rags. Nothing will ruin my day, because after school I have a date with Kyle. I'll get to see my other dog, Beauty, and Rollerblade down the path near Little Stone Bridge. Nothing can ruin that.

Is Mom a mind reader or what? Because the next thing she says to me is, "Could you come straight home after school in case Debra's late from her appointment and Teal has to leave daycare?"

She looks at me expectantly.

I keep from screaming by counting to ten and taking deep calming breaths.

"Why would Teal have to leave daycare?" I ask quietly.

"If he's sick," Debra explains. "I'm sure it's just the teething, but he feels a bit warm."

"I'm meeting someone at five. I can't be stuck with the brat today."

"Elizabeth! Don't call Teal a brat. He's your nephew. You can still make your five o'clock date. Debra's just going for a lunch downtown, but we can't count on traffic."

"Fine, I'll come straight home."

For the third time, I'm a *good girl* for my sister. No way am I going to be in a bad mood over anything, I vow as I head outside. It's a bright, cool day, a day of opposites, mellow yet crisp. I whistle on the way to Alicia's house. Smiling, I tell her my good news as she steps out the door.

"So he finally called after all this time and you said yes? What happened to our deal?" Alicia asks me as we walk up the sidewalk together.

"It's just a date. Single dates are allowed."

We walk quickly under the clear blue sky, perfect weather for Rollerblading.

"I'm not going to go *out* with him."

"Sure Liz, sure."

She rolls her eyes. "And you won't go all gaga over him like you did with Scott. You absolutely promise."

"Of course. I made him wait a few days for the date."

Truth is I already feel more attracted to Kyle than I ever did to Scott. Maybe it's because of Beauty. And this perfect weather seems to forecast a perfect date.

"Good." Alicia chucks me on the shoulder. "So don't blow it and act too eager."

I shake my head and sigh.

"You know I don't even see Kyle all day unless I hunt him down. And I've resisted over the past few days."

"Good work. Let him make all the moves. And I want you to know..." she wags her finger at me now, "since our deal allows single dates, I'm calling Scott tonight."

"Whatever." Clearly, it's impossible to keep Alicia away from him.

The day drags, and I find it hard to concentrate in class. No sightings of Kyle in the hallways, and I keep checking the clock. When the day finally ends, I race home. Magic greets me from her crate with a thumping tail.

"Come on, girl, you can come to the park too."

She follows me up to my room, and I pile my helmet and knee and wrist guards on my unmade bed while I rummage for a cleaner top in the pile on the floor. I change quickly but when I'm done, my wrist guards have disappeared.

"That's funny. I'm sure I put them right here." When I can't find something, and I talk out loud, I feel more in control, like I'm not going totally insane.

A few seconds, later Magic nudges me from behind, holding the wrist guards in her mouth.

I can't help laughing.

"All right, then. You carry them."

I scoop up the skates and kneepads. We head down the stairs together just as the front door opens. In comes my worst nightmare: Rolph, hair slicked back, tie knotted loosely around his collar—Teal under his arm.

"Elizabeth, emergency. Teal has a fever, and I had to pick him up from daycare. You have to watch him."

"Sorry. I'm going out." I try to squeeze past them at the door.

Rolph cuts me off with his body.

"I have an appointment in ten minutes for a large contract, and I should have already left for it."

Teal starts screaming loudly.

"Where's Debra?" I shout over the din.

"Still at lunch with her editor."

"But it's 4:30. Nobody can eat that long."

"I know. I thought she'd be back by now. She may be home any moment. Please, please, little sister, you must watch your nephew just till then."

"I've got a date. And I'm going to be late."

I recognize the look on his face too late. His mouth sets and his eyes shift. In a lightning move, he dumps Teal on the floor and dashes out the door, slamming it behind him. My mouth drops open in disbelief.

"You can't do this to me!" I yell at the closed door. "I hate you; I hate you; I hate you!"

CHAPTER 8

Kyle and Beauty

"How ya doin', man?" Ryan joins me at my table during lunch break. The chair beside me scrapes back.

"Heard you took on old man Veen in English class the other day." He slaps my back. "Didn't think you had it in you."

"You like that, do you?" I grin. It's good that he thinks I can stand up for myself.

"Didn't do me much good though. I still have to read a mouldy oldy, only now I have to *compare and contrast* it to a Nobel prize winner."

"Well, it wasn't the brightest thing to do, but that's part of what I like about it," Ryan answers.

Beauty shuffles at my feet. I snap into my last carrot stick. I've finished all the salad and other vegetables Mom packed for me, and as I sip at my sugar free pop, I feel pretty good. My day's only going to get better too, because at five o'clock I will be Rollerblading with a girl whose voice lifts me to a higher plane.

On the bus home, Donald sits with Beauty and me again. I try to ignore him and listen to that *Blindness* book on CD but he keeps tapping at my arm to talk to me. He's all excited about some boyfriend of his mom's promising to sign him up for hockey, and he jabbers away. I get the idea there's no dad at his house, or other kids.

"Can you play hockey?" Donald asks me.

I give up and take off my earphones. "No, but I'm going Rollerblading with a friend today."

"Aw, you're lucky. I've always wanted to Rollerblade but my mom thinks it's too dangerous. She probably won't even let me play hockey."

I chuckle to myself. His mom thinks Rollerblading is too dangerous—mine lives in fear of me even crossing a street by myself—makes the whole idea so much more thrilling.

As we approach my stop, Donald tells me he lives near the park. Maybe he'll see me there later.

"Not if I see you first," I joke.

"Huh?"

"Never mind—just remember you have to come over to me to say 'hi'. I can't see you. Forward, Beauty."

Beauty and I get off the bus. I shiver and throw my jacket on. It's gotten that much cooler.

Five blocks later, I'm home. I'm in a hurry, so I skip the testing and inject four units of insulin—for a glass of milk and a couple of Arrowroot biscuits, that should be about right. Of course, with Rollerblading, I might need less insulin; I decide as I eat. I'm thirsty and milk's usually a good stabilizer so I have another glass. Shawna and I head out together because she's off to a friend's house. It's past the park so she leads the way for Beauty and me. Beauty acts more like a plow horse than a dog guide . Can't she behave around any girls?

Never mind, I think. A brisk walk will keep my levels right, and I'll be at the park early, too. The sun shines warm on my face despite the nip in the air—summer struggling to hang on for another afternoon.

"I'm going to sit near the swing," I tell Shawna, and I put my headset on to listen to more of that awful book, *Blindness*, as I wait.

In the book, more and more people are losing their sight, and all are sent to an institution because whatever they have is contagious. The blindness spreads to everyone anyway, and society breaks down. That makes it easy to compare with *Lord of the Flies*. It's as though blindness represents death to mankind. Let's face it, that's what sighted people think anyway. One of the soldiers in the book shoots himself when he catches the disease. They'd rather be dead than blind. Isn't that the way I once thought, too?

I smile because something is different now. I'm close to being happy. I feel like I absorb life now through my skin, inhale it through my nose. Whatever shape and form I can experience life in, I certainly don't want to give any of it up.

What time is it? My watch says 5:15. Where is Elizabeth? Could I have missed her with this headset on? Beauty stirs at my feet. Maybe I couldn't see or hear her, but Beauty sure would have let me know.

Fifteen minutes isn't that long, I tell myself. Anything can make you that late. Some people are just chronically late anyway. I don't know that much about Elizabeth. Maybe she's one of those people.

The sun's warmth suddenly evaporates. A cloud blocking the sun? I stand up and feel a shudder through me. Elizabeth doesn't want to go out with a blind guy. Who am I kidding? By 5:30, she still hasn't shown. She's sent her message clearly. *I feel sorry for you, so I can't say no, but I won't show, and you'll get the hint.*

I stand up to pace with Beauty, and a familiar voice calls to me. It's Donald.

"Hey, Kyle, did you Rollerblade yet? Where's your friend?"

"I don't know, Donald. She never showed. I have no idea what happened."

"Where does she live? Do you wanna go over there and check?"

A kid's question, direct and simple. And I answer straight from my gut.

"Yeah. I want to do that. Can you help me find her address?"

CHAPTER 9

Elizabeth and Magic

The doorbell rings. Teal wakes up. I run to the door, hoping it's Debra.

Oh my God, it's him—tall, broad shouldered, and slim, spiked dark hair, his blue eyes reflecting an ocean of possibility as they gaze upwards. Except for a beige tee shirt thrown over his other top, he's dressed all in black. The sight of him sucks my breath away as I stare up at him.

Below, at our knees, the two dogs face off, Beauty snarling, Magic standing her ground. My attention shifts downwards. Does Beauty view Magic as a threat, as her replacement? Her head is low, her chocolate fur looks smooth and glossy compared to Magic's ruffled beige coat. They both have the same golden eyes but Beauty's, rimmed with pink, have taken on a greenish tinge. They look jealous. My mouth drops open in shock for a moment. Then I spring to action.

"Shush, Magic. Crate!" I snap my fingers.

Kyle yanks back at Beauty, hard. She stops growling, but looks up towards me and pants, tongue sliding in and out almost to the floor.

I squirm under her green-eyed stare. I'm not supposed to even talk to Beauty while she's still in harness. I can't think of anything to say to her.

"So you're not sick or dead or anything? Why'd you stand me up?"

Hurt, flat, and annoyed, Kyle's voice doesn't match the look in his eyes. They still gaze openly and optimistically towards the sky.

My skin flames up hot as Teal's.

"I'm so sorry..." I give Kyle the long explanation of why I got stuck babysitting, the words stumbling over one another. I sound guilty, rather than happy to see him. Does he believe me or not?

Teal's face breaks open in a yowl. Then it scrunches up around the effort of crying.

"Is that the baby?" Kyle asks, his lips lifting at the corners in a quarter smile.

"Uh huh. Sorry."

Kyle's smiling. He doesn't mind the wailing? I sway from side to side, bouncing Teal from hip to hip.

"Shh. He doesn't usually cry like this, but he's sick and I don't know what to do."

Kyle drops Beauty's harness and reaches out his arms.

"Can I hold him?" he whispers as though in a church. "I used to be the only one who could get my sister to stop crying when she was a baby."

"Sure! Come in, come in!"

I hand him Teal who's really screaming by this time, but Kyle grins openly. Then he calls behind him, to some kid on the sidewalk,

"It's okay. I can take it from here."

I step around him to push the door closed, unbuckle Beauty's harness and lead Kyle by the elbow into the living room. Beauty runs to the crate to challenge Magic, and they wrestle for a few moments, rolling around on the floor. Magic yips her defeat and Beauty, realizing that she's only a big puppy, lets her off. I pull Magic away, guide her into the crate and shut the door.

"There, there, hush," Kyle says to Teal, and his crying turns into softer hiccupping. "He feels like he's burning up. We used to give Shawna Tempra when she had a fever. Do you have any?"

"I'll check the medicine cabinet."

I dash to the bathroom with Beauty following behind me, just like old times. Nothing there.

"Maybe it's in Teal's room," I call.

I run towards the kitchen, down the stairs, through the TV/laundry room to Teal's room. The medicine's in a tiny red bottle with an eyedropper top, labelled with a baby picture—I know I've seen it. Ah ha! There it sits, on Teal's bureau.

I snatch it up and head back with Beauty.

"Found it," I tell Kyle and suction up the two millilitres the instructions suggest. I stick the dropper in Teal's mouth and squeeze the bulb handle.

"That's it."

"There, there," Kyle repeats to Teal and begins singing a lullaby, soft and low.

Teal reaches his tiny hand to touch Kyle's mouth as though amazed. Kyle purses his lips to kiss his fingers.

Wow. The dude with the attitude turns into a whole different person around babies. There's such tenderness as he continues singing. I'm melting as I watch Teal fall back asleep.

"His bedroom is in the basement," I whisper.

"Can we just stay here? We don't want to chance waking him, do we?"

I lead him to the couch where we sit down together. With one hand he pats the air in front of his feet.

"Where's Beauty?"

"Next to me. She doesn't have her harness on, so that's okay, isn't it?"

"Not really." He snaps his fingers at his feet, and Beauty looks up.

"Go, girl," I tell her.

"She's my dog."

"Sorry. Just trying to help."

"I have to do it myself."

His voice snaps just as his fingers did a second ago. Beauty moves over to his feet and looks up at him for praise. Nothing. She glances my way.

I nod and smile silently at her. Finally Kyle reaches down again and strokes her. Beauty settles.

"She loves music," I tell him. "She must love your singing. What is that lullabye? Can you teach it to me?"

"My mom used to sing it to me, and I sang it to my sister when she was scared of thunder storms." Kyle starts:

Sunshine and starlight
Reflect in your eyes
When you smile at me baby,
The clouds leave the skies

The world can be a dark place
Full of thunder, full of rain,
Life can bring hardship,
Love can bring pain

But I will love you always
You can close your sweet eyes
And I'll protect you baby
Till once again you rise

I sing it with him the next time through and then, with Teal tucked between us, round cheek against Kyle's chest, sleepered toes across my legs, Kyle fumbles for my chin with his hand. I lean forward, and we kiss.

No, no! Alicia and I agreed we wouldn't do this—fall for one guy, especially not this hard and fast. But my body liquefies, and my lips are the only things that can move. I don't even want to breathe or swallow.

From somewhere at the back of another world I hear a door open.

"Elizabeth, what are you doing?"

"Mom, you're home," I sputter as Kyle and I break apart.

"I thought for sure Debra would beat you."

"Clearly."

She drops the stack of books in her arms on the floor so she can dig her fists into her hip. Mom's wearing an army-green skirt and jacket, and she looks like a drill sergeant.

"Give me that baby." She steps toward Kyle, arms reaching as though she's going to strangle someone.

"He was sick and Rolph stuck me with him so he could go to an appointment."

Mom is about to explode. "Just give me the child."

Kyle lifts Teal up, and she takes him.

"Look at him. He's all flushed."

"His fever's coming down," Kyle tells her.

"Who are you?" Mom doesn't even let him answer but turns to me.

"What's got into you? This is a sick child."

"Mrs. Kerr, I'm sorry. I'm Kyle Nicholson. We haven't met before. I just stopped in to make sure Elizabeth was all right. We had a date to meet in the park and she never showed."

Mom turns into a witch woman, her eyes narrow into slits, her mouth bunches into a prune.

"Oh, so then you'd have been necking in public, I suppose."

I hate her, hate her, hate her. My hands bunch into fists.

"Why do you do this to me?" I yell. "I'm the one stuck babysitting the brat. I'm not the one who produced him."

She yells right back.

"But you know the rules. No boys in the house when you're alone. For heaven's sakes, Elizabeth, do you want to end up like your sister?"

At that point, the door suddenly opens again—Debra this time—my luck she has to arrive after Mom. She's wearing her dreamy I'm-on-another-planet look. She can't have heard any of our arguing. She also looks beautiful, with her hedgehog hair and plum-coloured full lips. Her top is plum, too, with an interesting cut-out neckline. After the baby, Debra actually developed cleavage, and it's on display today.

"How did your lunch go?" Mom instantly switches back to a normal person. I turn into the witch.

"Excuse me! Debra's gone till 6:00 for a lunch appointment, and I get yelled at for kissing a guy?"

Mom and Debra ignore me, as always.

"The art editor only had a few minor suggestions. Then he gave me a tour of the publishing house."

"What took you so long?" I shriek at her, and she blushes. That blush tells everything. The editor must have been cute. I turn to Mom.

"Just look at her face. Deb went out on a date, and she's the one with the kid."

"But she's twenty years old, and I didn't catch her necking on the couch just now, did I?"

"Elizabeth, can you just show me out?" Kyle interrupts. His face looks splotchy with red, like Teal's.

I cringe to realize how much our shrieking must have embarrassed him.

"Sure. We're leaving," I say, touching his arm.

I pick up Beauty's harness for Kyle, who snaps her back in. Beauty looks at me almost as long and hard as Mom. House of shrieking arguments or not, she still wants to stay behind. I step towards the door.

"You're not going anywhere!" Mom grabs my arm but I fling it off.

"Try and stop me!"

"Don't worry about it, Liz." Kyle reaches into his

pants pocket and pulls out a phone. "I'll call my sister."

I can't give in to the witch woman. I open the door and call Beauty to go forward.

"She's my dog! I give the commands," Kyle says.

I walk out first, with Beauty and Kyle following.

"Geez, I know you're mad at your mom, but do you have to put me in the middle?"

"I...I'm sorry." There's a catch in my voice so I guess Kyle realizes I'm crying.

"There, there."

He talks softly as he reaches for my face with his hands. They land, and with his thumbs he rubs the tears from my cheeks.

"Families are all crazy in their own way."

"Never like mine. My sister always causes these dramas. And my parents take it out on me."

"It's no fun causing the drama, either." Kyle shrugs. "Trust me, I know."

"I...I'm sorry."

"Don't be."

He brings his mouth to mine a second time. If Mom steps out now, I will be grounded forever. But I don't care. His lips are so soft, and mine turn into mush beneath his. I can't even breathe.

Chapter 10

Kyle and Beauty

When you go blind, people think you automatically hear better but it's not true. Nothing improves. My diabetes is still as bad as ever and so are the mood swings that result from it. But since I've accepted my blindness—well maybe, since I got Beauty—the rest of my senses seem hungrier. I love to listen to beautiful sounds: the water tumbling over the rocks at Little Stone Bridge in the park, my knife scraping across the toast as I butter it, and the coffeemaker heaving and sighing as it brews. And Elizabeth's voice.

I also love the feel of her face, her skin, warm and smooth, and her lips. When we kiss, it just opens one long ache that throbs right through me, and my skin wants more. Like an amoeba that eats through its pores, I want to feel Elizabeth close to me all over.

Elizabeth walks me to the bus stop.

"If you want to drop the harness and use the leash, I can guide you," she suggests.

"No! Beauty guides me."

What is wrong with me? I can hear the bite in my tone and feel the edginess inside me. Irritation crawls under my skin; do I need more insulin? Why now? I put my hand out to touch her and find calm again. It lands on her shoulder.

"Can I hold your hand?"

No answer. What is she thinking?

"Don't nod, I can't see you!" The bite turns sharper.

"Sorry, sure." Her small hand slips into mine—instant soothing warmth.

"Forward, Beauty. Forward, I mean it."

I feel the dog turning in her harness to look at Elizabeth. I don't want her to look elsewhere for my commands. I rattle at her harness harder than ever before. She finally moves. I want to scratch everywhere. What is wrong with me? Then it comes to me. I ate more snack than usual so my blood sugar wouldn't crash while we Rollerbladed. Of course—all I ended up doing was sitting, singing, and kissing. I'll have to give myself more insulin. A regular guy out with his girl, what I wouldn't give if I could just be that.

"Can we try Rollerblading tomorrow?" I ask when we arrive at the bus stop.

"Mom's home then. I'd love to, only can we make it next week?"

She's delaying, does she really want to go? Is she playing hard to get?

"Mom works late in the afternoons so she won't have to know."

There's a pleading note in her voice, she must want to try again. I smile through the edginess and nod.

"Can you give me your cell number in case something comes up again?" she asks me.

The bus rumbles up, squealing, and puffing out hot diesel fumes as I tell Elizabeth the number. Beauty doesn't want to move again. She hates buses anyway.

"Find the door, Beauty. Now! Forward. Come on!"

I climb the steps and end up standing all the way home with her, squeezed between rush-hour commuters. At least that's extra exercise, maybe that will bring my level down. It's all I can do not to elbow everyone away from us.

We get home after the usual five-block walk. I should be glad I can do it myself—last year, it would have been impossible. But Mom is already waiting, sounding almost as annoyed as I feel.

"I came home early with your book so we could start reading. Where were you?"

"Just out, Mom."

The book, *Blindness*, the swearing incident with Mr.

Veen, I've forgotten all about them. Spending time with Elizabeth has put it all out of my mind till this minute.

"You went out by yourself. How would I know that you even made it home alive?"

"I walked with Shawna. Didn't she tell you?"

"She's not home either."

"Well, we would have left you a note but how could we know you'd be home?"

"Never mind that now. Hurry and sit down. Maybe we can get through the first two chapters before supper."

"No. Honestly, Mom. Not now."

"What's wrong? Did you have your snack? You sound funny."

I hate the way Mom almost knows from my voice that something's wrong.

"Nothing. I'm fine. Okay. Let's read and get this over with."

Any voice usually reads with more passion than Perfect Paul, the one I've selected on my screen-reading program, but Mom's voice sounds flat. Is she still annoyed with me? She's reading quickly, too, like she needs to get it over with—and, let's face it, Mom always has a million things to do. Then I hear the edge creeping into her voice. She can't believe what's happening in the plot. She's zipping along as fast as she dares, but the story line upsets her as much as it does me, and she breaks down and finally asks, "Why do you want to read this book again?"

"Because it's a Nobel Prize-winner. No one can argue that it's not literary enough. I'm going to ace English and get into Queens, Mom. And there's another reason."

"I'm listening." Then the phone warbles, and I know I've lost her attention.

"Go ahead and answer it," I tell her, irritated.

Hearing only Mom's side of the conversation, I still know it's Elizabeth's mother on the other end.

"My son would never...I raised him to be a gentleman!" The rising pitch of Mom's voice tells me Liz's mother is getting to her.

When she hangs up, she turns to me.

"That was your new friend's mother. You're to stay away from her. She's too young for you. And just to help you with that, I'm grounding you—two weeks. I'll call home at 3:45 every day, to make sure you're at home doing your homework the way you're supposed to be on a week night."

"You're just using this as an excuse. You'll feel really safe if I'm tied down to house, won't you?"

"I never feel safe about you, but let's be clear about this. That girl's mother doesn't want you anywhere near her daughter. And you have an English project to finish, so no arguing. Now go take your insulin."

I stomp off into my room and kick the bureau in frustration. The clinkety clatter of my needles spilling from their jar reminds me, just like Mom's nagging voice, that it's blood testing time. I scoop them up and stuff all but one back in their place. I use that needle to prick the side of my index finger and bleed into my glucometer—only to find that, yes, I need some extra units of insulin. How much of my anger is real? I wonder as I lift my shirt and inject myself with a syringe. Who knows? I wait a few minutes and then call Liz on the phone. Her voice sounds sad, and I tell her about my 3:45 curfew.

"If we had a car, we could still Rollerblade and make it," she tells me.

"Neither of us could drive it though," I remind her.

She chuckles, happy bubbles of sound, and it doesn't seem so bad. I promise Liz we'll find a way. We'll work things out.

Her voice drops.

"My father's home. Do you have an MSN address? I'm not sure I can call you anymore."

I give it to her, and she hangs up. The click sounds so final, but Elizabeth likes me so I won't let myself feel bad. Instead, I grab my guitar and strum, shifting my fingers from chord to chord. That always helps. Beauty's muzzle anchors itself on my knee—that feels good, too. She loves music—C, G, F—I love the guitar, too, and I hunt for the combination of chords that most resembles Liz's voice.

The feeling overwhelms me again. The one that makes me want to absorb Liz right into my skin. I put together words.

I want to be closer
To feel your skin breathe into mine
To have your heart beat out my rhythm
And make you all mine…

It's probably wrong to feel this way. She's too young for me, as Ryan says. Everything about Liz feels so right to me, though, like she's everyone I've ever wanted. I loved Maddie, for sure, but this love is different. It's like I've been swallowed. I sing my words over a few times, strumming different chords till my fingers hurt.

A soft chime from my computer signals I have an instant message. Is it her? I feel a rush just at the possibility so I switch on Perfect Paul to read the message to me.

"Comatose King: Hey, Music Man, Party time this weekend. Up to a beer run?"

In Perfect Paul's voice, Ryan sounds calm and reasonable. I type back: *Music Man: Busted for seeing Liz. Can't make it.*

"Comatose King: Bummer! How's next weekend look?"

Grounded for 2, no can do. But the suds. We can buy them at lunch, Friday. You can drive.

Ryan's dad lets him use his 2003 Mustang convertible all the time. He's actually going to give it to him if he graduates from high school this year. But what's even cooler is that Ryan lets me drive it, in the church parking lot. Well, it's usually in exchange for buying the party beer. We have this whole beggar-boy routine going. I stand in front of the beer store wearing my big black shades and looking lost. Then I pester some sucker into buying us a two-four. You don't want to ask a blind kid for ID, after all. I hate doing it but love driving.

Then it hits me like a lightning bolt: I'll swap a different kind of favour.

Music Man: Don't want to drive. Will take a lift to the park instead. Me and Liz.

"Comatose King: Red-haired Girl. All right, Music Man. See you Monday."

Next I key in Elizabeth's addresses.

Music Man: Liz, it's me, Kyle.

I'm lucky. She's on the computer.

"Red: Hi, Kyle, waz up."

It's a shock hearing her words from Perfect Paul.

Music Man: Bring the Rollerblades to school next Friday. I've found a way.

CHAPTER 11

Elizabeth and Magic

Back from walking with Kyle to the bus stop, I overhear Debra talking to Mom as I walk through the door.

"I can't believe you'd let her go out with a blind guy. What does she even see in him?"

The whole day's events boil up inside me and I explode.

"Why don't you mind your own business?"

I barrel into the kitchen to let Magic out of her crate. She wags her tail and stands up immediately, but I'm too angry to pat her. She chases after me as I rush into the living room.

"I had a date to go Rollerblading with Kyle. You dumped me with your kid, so I couldn't go."

"You can't take him Rollerblading. He'll kill himself," Rolph interrupts from the sidelines.

I glance away from Debra to Rolph, who's leaning

back on Dad's reclining chair, hands behind his head, so comfortable—too comfortable.

"Elizabeth, it's not that he's blind," Mom says. "This boy is too old for you!"

She's perched on the edge of the couch beside Debra. Both of them hold cups of tea. Debra also has a nursery monitor in her lap. Oh, sure, for them Teal sleeps quietly in his crib.

"Kyle's seventeen. Come on Mom, Dad's three years older than you!"

"That's different!" She clatters her teacup down on the coffee table.

"Why?"

"Be reasonable." Mom hisses like a snake coiled to attack. "We wouldn't put Teal in junior kindergarten with four-year-olds. When you're young, three years makes a huge difference."

"What? Are you saying I'm a toddler?"

"No, what she's really saying..." Rolph butts in, "is that he's only in it for sex."

"Shut up! Not everyone's like you. Why are you even here? My sister has a new boyfriend, or hasn't she told you?"

Rolph pitches forward. Debra shrieks.

"Elizabeth! Go to your room." Mom flings up her arm, pointing out the direction, as though I don't know the way.

"Gladly. Come on, Magic." I stomp off, with Magic trotting behind me.

She's not supposed to jump up on furniture, but once in my room I throw myself onto my bed and pat the spot beside me. What can it hurt? She's not going to be guiding herself, and it's not like her puppies will inherit the tendency.

Magic licks at my face till I finally pull away, rubbing my own sleeve across my drooly wet cheeks and chin. How can you stay upset with a dog's face right in yours, watching your every eye-blink and expression change? I stroke her golden head as I lie back and contemplate the ceiling. I play and replay conversations with my mother, or Rolph, or Deb. In all of them, I end up ahead with the last word, and they realize how wrong they are. It gets dark in my room, and I don't have the energy to get up and switch on the light. I doze slightly.

The phone rings. Magic's ears lift, and I rub the tip of one between two fingers as I pick up the portable from my desk. It's Kyle. He tells me my mother called his, and I want to kill her all over. But I continue to feel the velvety soft tip of Magic's ear and to grit my teeth. Her head angles to one side.

"I've been grounded for two weeks so I can concentrate on my comparative essay. Really, I need so much extra time to do my homework. It's probably for the best."

"My mother teaches English at Sheridan College," I tell Kyle. "She could have helped you write a killer essay."

"What, you think I can't do it by myself?"

He's silent for a moment, then apologizes. "I'm sorry. Sometimes when I don't get my insulin dose just right, I get irritable."

"Why don't you test your blood sugar more often?"

Kyle sighs. "It just plain hurts my fingers, and after, it's hard to play guitar."

"Can't you test some other place?"

"My toes or my ears. But I have to watch for sores, especially on my feet. Diabetics have poor circulation and get infections easily. I'd rather die than lose a leg. And—obviously, I can't see to check my feet over routinely."

I don't know what to say about that. If I had a choice over losing my legs or my vision, I think I'd choose a leg. Once I was blind, I can't imagine losing a leg or anything else could ever be as big a deal.

Kyle continues. "Listen, I'm sorry, I don't mean to load all this on you. It's something I'm working on. You're important to me, and I don't want anything to get between us."

Too late, Mom's right there already, I think. I feel so connected to Kyle. I can only hope that my sister Deb distracts Mom's attention with all her drama so that

I can see him again.

"You're...important to me too."

Magic barks, and I hear the garage door opening. Dad's home. I know he'll be sent up to talk to me, which makes me want to get off the phone in a hurry. It's hard to pay attention to what Kyle's saying anymore, I'm so distracted. I cut the conversation short and slam down the receiver as louder discussions start in the kitchen.

"She said *what* to him?" Dad hollers.

Murmur, murmur, murmur is the answer. Magic's ears perk up, and my fingers slip from the one I was rubbing. Dad's stomping down the hall.

"I won't let them get to me. Don't worry, girl. It's all good. For the first time in my life, I have a dog I can keep. And a boy that I think I can love forever."

My father knocks on the door.

"Elizabeth, may I come in? I have to speak to you."

"Okay."

I'd rather talk to him than Mom—although, no contest, she's the boss. Anything Dad and I agree on will have to be cleared with her later.

Dad walks in, still dressed in his business casual: a red golf shirt and navy wrinkle-free slacks. He sits on the bed, squeezing onto a small space left by Magic, smiling and patting her. No one can stay mad if they pat a dog.

"She's a real beauty, isn't she?"

I shrug. With her golden fur and eyes, Magic is classically beautiful. Beauty, the Chocolate Lab had—has—an odd look, with her pink lips, gums and eyelids. Still I'd feel disloyal favouring this dog's looks over Beauty.

"It's all about what's inside." I sit up and pat Magic too. "Isn't that what you and Mom always say?"

"Look at her eyes. Don't you think Magic is beautiful on the inside, too?" Dad asks.

"Yeah, probably. I just don't know her as well as Beauty yet."

"Speaking of which, do you think it's a good idea for you to see her new owner?" Dad asks me, looking directly into my eyes. Flecked with brown, his irises look just like mine.

"He's not her owner—he's her handler. Canine Vision Canada owns all the dogs."

Dad keeps looking at me patiently, and then I break from the stare and glance down.

"His name is Kyle. Beauty will adjust. She'll learn to concentrate even when I'm around."

"Mmm. Shouldn't she already know how, by now? Isn't that what they train the dogs to do at Canine Vision?"

I look back up at him and raise my voice.

"I can't always give up everyone I love. I don't want to give up Kyle, and I don't want to stop seeing Beauty."

Dad speaks even more calmly.

"You're going to have to, Elizabeth. Your mother will

not allow you to go out with this boy."

"That's not fair!" I punch the bed hard, and Magic jumps up.

"If I hadn't got stuck babysitting today, she would have never known about him."

"But now we all know," Dad answers, no change in his tone.

"You can't let her do this! I didn't want to watch the brat today. I didn't have any say. I'm always stuck with everyone else's choices!"

"If you're talking about Debra, that's another issue. Teal must see his father. We're all stuck with that."

"Exactly!"

"But we want to take care that Rolph sees him on our terms—not that he fights to get him on a more permanent basis. To mention a new boyfriend to him, real or imagined, wasn't a smart thing to do."

"I know. He just made me so mad. He's always hanging around, and now he's telling me what to do. He's the one who really got Mom going. He said Kyle was only interested in me for sex."

"Well, you're certainly too young for that, Elizabeth."

Dad sounds less calm now, angry even. Why? What have I done? Nothing—it's all about what Debra did, and what they assume I might do, too. He lectures on.

"You're only fifteen. Come on, what is he, in his

final year? Your mom said he looked older, more mature..." Dad trails off.

"So you think Rolph's right—the only reason a seventeen-year-old would go out with me is for sex."

"Not the only reason."

"Dad, I'm going to keep seeing him."

"Not for the next two weeks you're not. You're grounded. And no boys in the house when you're alone. You know the rules."

I look at Dad, bald, wrinkled, and beaten. I purse my lips. I could live with the grounding and the no-boys-in-the-house rule—but Mom said something else. She won't let me go out with Kyle ever. If I have to break one rule, I may as well break them all. And the good thing about Mom's teaching at the college is that she has late classes every day. If I time my Rollerblading correctly, so I'm home by six, she'll never have to know I've seen Kyle at all.

Chapter 12

Kyle and Beauty

Friday—Mr. Veen hands out sheets with due dates on them. By next week, we have to decide on our theme for our study. By the week after, we have to have the introductory paragraph written. For the third week, we have to have topic sentences and supporting facts. Then we have another month to hand it in. Can people really write like this? Why does he have to break up the whole project into a math formula? Math, the subject I hate. There's only one way I can handle this assignment. I have to write the whole thing first and then give him his lines week by week. It means I have to read the book faster and work harder than anyone else.

I groan, and Beauty jumps up, paws on my knee.

"It's all right, girl. Don't worry, I'm fine."

It feels like my whole future hangs on this one class, and whether I can keep up with it or not. Already I feel overwhelmed—down, down, at the bottom of a hole where I can't claw my way up. I'm just overtired, I'm sure. Do I need more carbs? Or less? It's such a pain.

"Forward, Beauty," I say at the end of the class.

We leave the room and Beauty barks, tail slapping wildly against my leg. Why is she so happy?

I smell a baby-sweet scent and smile as I feel Liz's lips on my cheek—soft and so gentle. It's been a whole week, like forever. I can't help myself, and I reach my arms around her and pull her close to me. What am I doing?

"Mr. Nicholson?" Damn, it's Old Man Veen. "Would you like to explain to the office why you feel this behaviour is appropriate in the school hallway?"

Is that a real question, or is he sending me to talk to the principal? I have to think quickly. What if they call Elizabeth's parents?

"Sorry, sir. It's a scene from Romeo and Juliet. We were just practising."

"Yes, well, I think you have it down perfectly now. No more practising in the hall."

"No, sir," I agree quickly and sigh with relief.

"Get to your next class."

"Yes, sir. Forward, Beauty."

Beauty seems to be drifting to one side. "No, girl, no!"

I turn to Elizabeth. "Walk with me," I whisper.

She slips her hand in mine.

"Meet me after school in the parking lot," I tell her. "We can ride to the park together. As long as I'm home by 3:45."

"I'm grounded, too. But that's okay, no one's around till 6:00 tomorrow. Mom will never know."

I get to my French class and drop Elizabeth's hand. Beauty pulls towards her.

"Stop! No!" I yank at her leash.

I reach out and catch Elizabeth's chin in my hand, leaning to kiss her. She pulls away quickly not giving me the chance.

"Meet you at my friend's car," I tell her. "You can't miss it. It's the only Mustang in the lot. Beauty, this way—no, forward."

I can understand how Elizabeth mesmerizes the dog. I feel like I'm walking on a different level myself. There's a layer of air between my feet and the ground.

"Beauty, I mean it now. Forward."

Finally, she behaves the way she's supposed to.

In French class, I get another novel to read. I put my hand up to call attention to my problem but after a second, I feel Madame Bouchard slipping what feels like an audiotape into my cassette player.

"From the Board office, for you," she says. "Le roman."

Not every teacher thinks I'm such a big inconvenience to teach. I sigh with relief and head for the door.

Ryan grabs me the moment I step into the hall.

"Let's go, Music Man. We have a date with the beer fairy."

"Yeah, yeah—let the dog do her job, will ya?" We take off down the stairs and out into the parking lot.

"High noon, warm day, let's open up the top."

By now, I know where to reach to pull the metal handle that unlocks the roof. There's a soft electric hum, and I feel the sun on my face. The brakes squeal as we take off. Freedom, the wind—I love Ryan's car. When we get to the beer store, the fun stops; it's humiliation time again.

I stand near the door, and Ryan whistles to let me know someone's close enough to hit on. It's a long whistle, so I know it's a guy. Darn, women are usually easier.

"Um, excuse me, sir. While you're in there, could you buy me a case of twenty-four? They won't let my dog in." It's a lie, but most people don't know the difference. Beauty growls softly.

"Don't I know you?" The guy's voice sounds familiar but I can't put a name to it. He snaps his fingers.

"You're Elizabeth's friend. I'm Rolph, her brother-in-law, sort of. You're old enough for beer, and you're hangin' around Liz?"

Well, I'm not old enough, obviously, or I'd be in there myself. I grit my teeth and say nothing.

"Sure, I'll get you some. Give me your money."

I hand him Ryan's cash, and Rolph is gone; it seems like forever. Finally, he slams a box into my chest. I grab a handle and let the case hang down heavy against my leg.

"Here. And your change."

I let go of Beauty's harness a moment so that I can hold out my hand. Then I tuck the coins he gives me back in my pocket.

"Look, Liz is really just a kid," Rolph tells me, like an older brother.

I grip the beer case tightly so that my hand bunches into a fist.

"Find somebody your own age. She's not your type."

"Right, Beauty." I wave my other hand in the direction she's supposed to go. "Find the car, girl."

"Good job." Ryan takes the case and stuffs it in the trunk, at least I hear the lid slam.

"Don't be mad. C'mon; it's over now. We've got our brewskies." I hear some bottles clinking.

"It's not that... Why does everyone make such a big deal over Liz being young?"

"I dunno. Maybe, 'cause you look older. Notice no one gives you a hard time about buying beer."

I hear him twist a bottle open and swallow.

"Ahh. She...well...she's eye candy, I'll give her that. But she's got that baby face, too." Ryan swallows again. "She looks more like a grade school girl."

"But there's nothing I can do about that."

"Got that right."

Another bottle twists open, and he puts it in my hands. "Might as well drink up and enjoy."

I hate when he drinks in the car, and I don't usually drink along with him anytime. It screws up my blood sugar—those sharp ups and downs could kill me. But now, in the middle of a school day, with the top down, I drink down the bitter suds—pure suicide. It feels right. There's so much I can't do about so many things. What's one bottle of beer in the bigger scheme of things?

When we're done, we head back to school, and I suffer through math and history a lot faster and easier knowing I'm seeing Liz afterwards.

At the end of the day, when I usually hang back until the halls have cleared for me to manoeuvre, I get Ryan to help Beauty and me get to the parking lot quicker.

"Do I look okay?" I ask him as we step out the doors.

"Perfect. And she's waiting. So smile."

I can't help but do anything else. It's like the sun is rising inside me. My skin turns warm and inside, my darkness brightens. Liz touches my arm, and my whole face cracks open into a grin.

"All set?" I ask.

"Brought the Rollerblades. I don't know if it will be like surfing in Hawaii, but that hill in the park makes for a great ride."

She remembers about my surfing in Waikiki from just

a couple of lines in the song I sang at Dog Guide graduation!

"If it even comes close, I'll be happy. It's not like I'll ever surf again."

"You don't think so?" Liz asks.

"I'll slide in the back to give you and Beauty room."

That's the trouble with the Mustang. It's a two-door with a really uncomfortable backseat. I consider sliding in beside her, but that would make Ryan the chauffeur. We take a while climbing in. Ryan slides the roof down again, but it's a little cooler this late in the day. As we drive, Elizabeth and I have to shout at each other in order to hear.

"You know some of the CNIB gang go downhill skiing, with two-way radios. I bet you can do that with surfing, too," she calls.

"Wow, that would be great." Maddie would have never suggested a thing like that. She was always trying to stop me from doing things that might get me hurt.

"Did you say it was too late?" Liz calls back to me.

"No, it would be great. To surf with radios I mean." She cups her hand to her ear.

"Never mind." We coast through the wind in silence now.

A few minutes later, Ryan parks the Mustang, and while I can take off my own shoes and stuff my feet into the boot of the Rollerblades, I can't do up the laces.

"Here, let me." I inhale her scent as I feel the boots tighten. When we're all done, I wonder what to do with Beauty.

"Why don't you take off her harness? Let her be a regular dog for a change."

"You know we're not supposed to, unless it's an enclosed area."

Still—a regular dog, I twinge at the phrase, and I unharness Beauty. Her tail slaps at my leg happily. It's obvious I stop her from having a regular life.

"She's good with Rollerblading, but we'll make her wait at the top of the hill so she doesn't trip us up. How do you want to do this? Want to hold my hand or grab onto my waist?"

"I like the waist idea."

She immediately puts my hands at the top of her hips, where there's a smooth curve. I take a deep breath to keep myself from sliding my hands up and down.

"You can just coast behind me, or push off to the side with each foot. Kinda like ice skating."

We start off, and it's all I can do at first, just to coast and feel the path rumble underneath my wheels. Liz gets ahead, making my arms stretch long, but then I push off and bump into her. It's like a lightning jolt along my body, wherever hers touches mine.

"Okay, now." I hear gentle laughter in her voice. "We're going up the hill, I need you to push."

My calves strain and burn as we climb upward.

"Beauty, stay," Liz says.

"I think you need to just hold my hand here, to get the full sensation." She pulls my hands off her waist and holds onto one. "Ready?"

"I guess." It's not like surfing at all, where I felt a rush of power under my feet that my balance controlled. I feel like I'm hurtling through time and space far too fast. Like the way I feel about Elizabeth.

"We're coming to the grate now. Hold on!"

I grip her hand tightly but when my wheels catch on the new surface I swing round and smack into Elizabeth hard. She falls backwards and I fall on top of her.

CHAPTER 13

Elizabeth and Magic

I tumble backwards, half on the pavement, half on the grass, and he lands on top of me.

My elbows smart, right through my jacket. My butt throbs. But none of that matters. It's the weight of Kyle on top of me that burns into me.

"Are you okay?" I gasp.

"Oh, yeah." He grabs my chin with his hand and smothers me with his kiss. He presses down on me even more, and I don't want to get up. I can feel my own heart beat, a slow hard pump, or is that his? Everything feels so good.

"Kyle, are you okay?" I hear a little kid's voice from a distance. "Your hand's bleeding."

Kyle lifts himself off me, and I see a boy about ten years old with pale skin and wide green eyes watching me suspiciously. He could be Kyle's younger brother, apart from the eye colour.

"Donald?" Kyle says, his voice husky.

Donald's dark hair sticks up a bit in the back and is badly in need of a cut. It gives him a neglected, forlorn look.

"I saw you fall. Does it hurt?" He points to Kyle's hand.

"No, it's nothing," Kyle answers. "I just landed on this bottle cap."

"But you're really bleeding!" I reach into my pocket for a tissue and press it to the wound.

"Oh, stop it! I've been around enough nurses in my life."

He shakes me loose and blood drips from his hand.

Donald looks on with eyes as wide as saucers.

"Kyle, keep the tissue on, please."

"Fine," he grumbles.

"You were kissing," Donald accuses us now.

"So what? Listen, don't you have kids your own age to hang with?"

Donald hangs his head and kicks at the ground but, of course, Kyle doesn't see the effect his words have.

"Hey, do you want to see Beauty do an Elvis impersonation?" I ask him.

"Yeah, sure," Donald answers.

"Okay, sing with me. 'You ain't nothing but a hound dog...'"

Kyle joins us, and he sounds just like Elvis. Beauty, on cue, waggles her butt and curls her lip over her incisor. Donald laughs and swivels his hips along with Beauty.

"She sure is a smart dog," he says when we're done.

"And Liz trained him; she owned him before me. Then she gave Beauty back to Canine Vision Canada, and they gave her to me."

"You gave up a smart dog like this?" Donald looks at me as if I'm crazy.

"Yeah, but now I'm friends with Kyle, and it doesn't feel like I've given her up at all."

Donald shrugs his shoulders. "Does she do other tricks? Can I throw a stick into the water and will she fetch it?"

"No," Kyle says sharply. "She's my dog and she's only supposed to do stuff for me." Kyle sounds like a different person suddenly, snappish and angry.

"Kyle?" I touch his arm.

"It's okay. I'm good. I've gotta get home now. I'll see you on the bus, Donald."

Kyle turns away from Donald who walks away, hands in his pocket.

"You kind of hurt his feelings," I say. I look back at Donald, shuffling across the path over Little Stone Bridge, head down, hands in his pocket.

"Well, he can't go on thinking I'm his best friend.

And I want to spend time with you, not him."

"It wouldn't have killed you to be nice to him. I used to always tag around with my sister, you know, looking up to her, wanting to be like her. I know what it's like to be treated like a pest."

"Ah, you're a big softie." He rubs my arm. "We'd better head back. It's almost time to go."

We skate back up the hill with Beauty still on the loose. She bounds along the grass at the side of the path, her tongue hanging sideways out of her mouth. I've been here a hundred times before, only now it's all different. The orange and red leaves seem brighter, the clouds more fluffy. The road under my wheels hums like it's happy, too. And the wind tugs gently though my hair. At the top, I hesitate for a moment. I've fallen on this hill a few times. Kyle smiles up at the sky. At least that's the way it seems because of the way his eyes look upwards.

We stop at a park bench for a last kiss.

Someone coughs nearby. "Well, just look at the time." Ryan interrupts us. "Did you say you had to be home for 3:45?"

It's already 3:40 on my watch. We quickly take off our Rollerblades and harness Beauty back up. We have to hope Kyle's mom doesn't call, bang on 3:45.

"Is it okay if he takes me home first, Liz?" Kyle asks as we settle back in the car.

"Sure. I'm going to beat my mother home no problem."

It doesn't feel as good taking Kyle home. With the top up, the car turns into a dark cave. I sit in the back, far away from Kyle. My elbows and my tailbone throb now from our fall, the skin around my mouth burns from Kyle's stubble scraping across it. Inside I feel a little dirty, like I've cheated on a test or stolen from the school Readathon money. Unfair as Mom is, I'm cheating on her.

But then the car stops, and Kyle gives me a long, gentle kiss before he leaves.

It's all good again.

Chapter 14

Kyle and Beauty

Back at home in my room, I try to scan the *Blindness* book into my computer. My mother will never have enough time to read the whole book to me. I work as fast as I can to make up for my time at the park, but my messenger dings, and I can't ignore it. Can it be Liz?

"Comatose King: Come to my party on the weekend. You know the girls love your music. My cousin's coming. You'll like her."

He's trying to run my life, just like my mother, making me give up Liz and go with someone else. Beauty snuffles into my hand, trying to pull my attention to her.

"I'm grounded. Remember? See ya."

I hit *Enter* and go back to scanning. It's such a time-sucking activity. Can I listen to the disk of *Lord of the Flies* at the same time? I just need a quick review of the book after all. Yeah, I decide, but as I fumble for the recorder in my backpack, the messenger dings again. Shut up Ryan, I think, but then I hear Perfect Paul read Liz's words.

"Red: Hey, Kyle, did you look after that cut?"

Just like Mom, just like Maddie, she's worrying about my health. Something flares up inside me. At least Maddie has an excuse, she wants to go into medicine, and Mom, well, she is my mother. I hit the keys angrily.

Music Man: Enough with the cut already, I'm fine.

Tape recorder in hand, I drape the headset over my neck while I paw my desk for the audiobook.

Perfect Paul starts up again.

"Red: Just wanted to remind you to clean it. That bottle cap looked pretty rusty."

Maybe if it was her voice talking to me I wouldn't feel so annoyed, but Perfect Paul lecturing me really grates. I ignore the message. The thing is, I didn't clean the stupid cut, and it does hurt. But I want to get this book scanned now, while I listen to the audio version.

"Red: So was Rollerblading like surfing?"

For a moment, I let myself go back to heaven, my hands on her waist, the movement under my feet, the wind against my face. My annoyance melts, and I tap out a message on the keyboard.

Music Man: Better. I was with you.

The phone rings, and I grope for the portable on my desk.

"Hi Kyle. I called earlier. Where were you?"

"Mom, couldn't find the phone, sorry," I lie. "What did you want?"

"To make sure you were home, obviously. Did you check your blood sugar?"

"Yup," I lie again, as I get out my kit.

"Good, don't forget your snack. Have you reviewed *Lord of the Flies*? You need to get at least one book done on your own."

"Doing that right now—you don't have to rag at me about everything. Gotta go, Mom. See you soon."

The moment I hang up, Perfect Paul talks at me again.

"Red: Do you want to go Rollerblading again Monday?"

I wince. I want to, but there's just so little time. As I think about it, I slip the audiobook into the player. I really don't have time for Liz. Especially since we have to sneak around parents. I have to get good grades. I have to do the mature thing. So I type: *Music Man: It's not a good idea. I'm swamped with my independent study.*

Then I angle the headset so that the earphones are in the correct position and turn off my messenger.

I hear a rhythmic ringing and wonder where it's coming from. When Shawna taps me on the shoulder, I jump.

"Phone for you. It's Elizabeth." She hands me the receiver.

"Kyle. Maybe I can help you with your homework?" Her words go up and down the scale, musical and gentle.

She can help me, that word. Just once, I want someone to need my help. I sigh.

"You're not answering. You just want to get rid of me, right? I get it now."

I can hear the hurt in her voice, a sharp trill in the middle of a line of music. So I explain about the three books I have to take in, somehow, over the next month.

"If that's really the problem, I'll read the book that you don't have the unabridged disk for." There's a tiny hitch in her breath as she waits for my answer.

If I say no, it will all be over, hearing her angel voice, kissing her soft lips, holding her smooth hand or her warm body. Her mom's already warned me off. She looks as young as Shawna, Ryan's told me. Ryan's just a jealous moron, I tell myself. And parents can't run your life.

"That would be great," I answer. "You could come home on the bus with me."

"Great. I can read for at least a couple of hours, and my mother will never have to know."

"All right, then. We have a plan. Bye."

She whispers a goodbye back to me. I smile. I feel like my ear has been kissed.

Just because they've been through a plane crash and are left on their own, does that mean the main characters have to behave so cruelly to each other? It's just like the *Blindness* book, where the inmates withhold food from one another. Why can't they stick together in times of trouble?

Ha! I have my thesis statement. I just have to word it correctly. I'm annoyed as I fumble for words in my head. Finally I type out the sentence and listen to Perfect Paul read it back. "In both *Lord of the Flies* and *Blindness*, disaster and isolation produce a separate, hostile society."

I still feel irritated. Oh, man—blood test, of course! I grab a tester needle from my bureau and prick the side of my right baby finger, the one least likely to see guitar strumming action. Then I squeeze it over the test strip I've inserted into the glucometer. Darn, I squeezed the bottle-cap cut and feel something trickle down my arm.

More blood? Shouldn't have trouble testing today. Still it takes a full minute till a voice tells me my level is high. No wonder I feel like an overdrawn elastic band. I inject the extra units of insulin into my stomach. My hand still feels wet, and I suck at the cut. Definitely bleeding—I have to get a bandage. I stand, and Beauty jumps up, anxious too, whimpering softly.

Her toenails click on the floor behind me as I head to the bathroom. I know where Mom keeps the bandages, on the top left shelf of the medicine cabinet. I get one out and manage to tear it open with my teeth—too hard to find the little tear string on the top. I taste bandage before I manage to get it out of the package and onto my finger. Medicine-flavoured plastic.

Everything goes back into the right place—bandages back in the box, box in the cabinet, mirrored door gets closed. I'm proud of myself. And I have my essay theme, too. Beauty bumps me from the side as I head back to my room. That dog just always has to lead.

A door slams, and I hear Mom calling out. She walks down the hall and then suddenly screams. "Oh my God! Kyle. Where are you? What's wrong? There's blood everywhere!"

Chapter 15

Elizabeth and Magic

When I get home, Magic goes nuts in the crate. I let her out and as I kneel down for my canine love fest, I wonder where everyone else is. Magic slaps her paws down happily in front of me, inviting me to play, and she wags herself crazy. I tousle the fur on her head, and she frantically licks my fingers.

"Poor dog, you've been so bored."

A noise from the basement makes Magic barks sharply. Burglars? I wonder.

"Shh, shh, Magic!" I open the door, and she bounds ahead of me down the stairs. Oh my gosh. What will we do if it is a break-in?

The first thing I see is the TV set turned on to some show with adults in children's clothing and clown make-up. They're skipping and waving their hands. Teal stands to the side, mouth open, eyes fixed on the screen, as his little hands hold onto the top of the set. Magic rushes over to him and accidentally knocks him down.

On the couch across from the set, Rolph lies curled up, snoring softly.

"What are you doing?" I yell close to his ear.

Teal uses the dog to pull himself back up.

"Huh, huh, what. Elizabeth? What time is it?" Rolph wakes and rubs his eyes.

"Teal can't just wander around while you sleep!" I tell him.

"Did I drop off? Teal was sleeping with me, I swear. He looked tired, so I lay down with him on the couch..."

"He has a nap every afternoon at daycare! The least you could do is let the dog out of the crate. Magic could watch him better than you do."

Magic's licking Teal's hands and face.

"Stop that dog. I don't want her to slobber on Teal."

I head over to the TV set, scoop Teal up, and stare at Rolph, wishing my sister had caught him, instead of me.

"Honestly, I just dozed off for a bit there..."

"Dozed off or passed out?"

He glares back at me. "Little Miss Perfect. I saw your boyfriend at the beer store. Wonder what your mother would say about underage drinking."

I dig a fist into my hip.

"I don't drink. Here, Pops," I drop Teal on Rolph's stomach, catching him off guard.

"Ooof," he gasps, and I disappear upstairs before he can stick me with Teal again. I message Kyle; his answers give me the strangest feeling—that he wants to get rid of me. I can't take it. I just have to call to hear him in person, to make sure I'm not getting confused signals.

He seems so stressed out by homework I still think he's making up excuses. But I didn't imagine his kisses, did I? We set up a reading date for Monday after school. Imagine, a reading date! I just have to consult with Alicia.

"I'm walking the dog," I call out.

It's a great excuse, in case I'm not back when Mom gets home. Grounded or not, I still need to take Magic out for tinkles. I leash her up, grab a jacket, and take off for Alicia's house. Ten minutes later, I knock on her door, and she opens it.

"Come in, come in. It's cold." She hugs herself and grins at me as Magic and I step into her front entrance. What's she so happy about?

I tell her all about my Rollerblading date, and then what just happened over messaging and the phone, asking for her interpretation of Kyle's words.

"I don't know, Liz. It sounds like he's playing games with you."

"What? But when he holds me, I know he cares. And

he wants me to read to him. What kind of game could that be?"

I want to smack Alicia for giving me the wrong interpretation—the one I didn't want to hear.

She just raises an eyebrow. "You see? This is why we swore off boys. They always muck with your head. Now you're mad at me."

"No, I'm not," I argue.

"Fine, have it your way." She grins again.

"Guess what? We're officially going out again."

"Who's we? You and Scott?" I ask.

"Of course, me and Scott. We were born to be together."

I roll my eyes. It's what I thought about Scott and me last year—something he encouraged me to think. He told me we'd get married at thirty, even though at the time he was going out with Gwen.

"Now that's someone who likes to play games," I tell her. Instantly, I realize I've said the wrong thing.

"You're just jealous!"

"No I'm not. I lo...ike Kyle, remember? Come on, walk with me. Magic's been in the house all day."

She folds her arms across her chest. "Can't. I'm waiting for a call from Scott."

"Oh, come on. That's what voice mail is for. You can call him back later."

"Oh, yeah? Well, maybe I need his help to do my

homework. He still has his project on Shylock from last year. Remember we were supposed to work on our Shakespeare together?"

"I'm sorry. I forgot. We can get on it over the weekend."

"Oh, sure. But you're grounded because of Kyle, remember? Let's face it. This guy is already getting in between us."

"And Scott never does that, right?"

Alicia doesn't answer, but we both know that Scott always causes the worst problems for everyone. And really, what kind of essay could he ever write? I feel sorry for Alicia.

"Well, okay. I'll see you on Monday." Magic and I leave again and continue our walk.

We end up, as usual, at Little Stone Bridge Park where I first met Kyle. I can almost see him sitting on that rock, dark glasses on, looking so cool—while I lay sprawled along the pavement. I hated him then—or was that just the flip side of love?

I unleash Magic and throw a stick for her, watching her golden ears trail behind her as she bounds after it. The joy on her face, the power in her stride, the satisfaction she gets from returning the stick lifts me, too. I can't help but feel happy. I remember doing the same thing with Beauty.

Does Beauty ever have fun like that with Kyle? I hope so.

A wind suddenly blows up, stirring dead leaves and dirt into a kind of mini-tornado—September warning about a colder month to come. I throw the stick for Beauty again.

"Hey, can I try that?"

I turn around and blink. "Donald? Did you get a haircut?"

"Yup," he answers.

But it's more than that. He's gelled his hair, and he's wearing all beige, except for a green tee shirt that he's layered over his beige top. Donald doesn't just look like Kyle's brother anymore. He looks more like a mini-clone of Kyle.

CHAPTER 16

Kyle and Beauty

"It's nothing, Mom, honestly. I tripped over the dog and fell on something." I couldn't admit I'd been Rollerblading to Mom.

"You and Beauty aren't adjusting that well at school."

"Sure we are!"

"Did you remember to disinfect the wound at least?" Mom asked and, really, how could I admit that I hadn't?

"Yeah, Mom, I did. The only thing I didn't do right, obviously, was clean up."

"Never mind—forget about it."

But over the next couple of days, the cut continues to bite and ooze. Nothing ever heals that quickly for me. By Monday, my hand and my head ache. I cancel on Liz and fall asleep on the bed the moment I get home.

Mom wakes me up. "Kyle, are you all right?"

She touches my forehead. "You feel warm. What's wrong?"

As she drops her hand, she accidentally brushes against mine making me wince. She has her answer.

"My God, Kyle, would you even notice if you had gangrene?"

She whips me off to the emergency clinic, and we wait a couple of hours in silence. I wish I'd brought one of my audiobooks, but I feel so worn out and limp that I'm not sure I could absorb any of the details. Slumping down on the vinyl chair, I hear the angry *flip, flip* of magazine pages. Sounds like she's not finding a lot that interests her, either.

Finally it's my turn, and of course she comes along, even though I'm almost eighteen. She talks to the doctor in front of me like I'm a child.

"Yes, he had his tetanus shot. I can't leave him alone for two minutes. This is what happens."

Her voice is exasperated. She can't do enough to keep me safe and healthy. She ends her sentence with her voice breaking. She sounds like she's close to tears.

"Diabetics have such poor circulation." The doctor clucks as she holds my hand and turns it over. "Their immune systems aren't great either."

It's like I'm some defective model of car. She hems and haws a moment, thinking out loud, that perhaps the hospital should keep me overnight and put me on an

IV so that the antibiotics can kick in quicker.

"Please, no. Give me an extra-strength pill, an injection, anything. I don't want to stay here."

There have been too many hospital stays for me. To lie in the dark alone somewhere unfamiliar, where Beauty can't lead me, and I can't stumble by myself—even to the bathroom. To hear noises that don't connect to me: gurneys squeaking down the hall, whispered discussions, random cries of pain, machines hissing as they breathe for someone. And the smell! Disinfectant and old blankets, soap and blood.

"Home can be the best medicine of all," the doctor relents. She's quiet, and I hear a tear of paper, the prescription.

My mother puts her arm around me, and we lean each against each other as we leave the hospital. She squeezes me, and I squeeze back. We're both very disappointed in my life, and in my health.

I take a double dose the moment the prescription is filled, but that simple infected cut lays me up for the whole week. No Elizabeth. She doesn't call, either, and anyway, I feel too sick to even pick up the receiver. It's as if my life energy ebbs away with each throb of my finger. I'm sure she doesn't care about me anymore, and then that thought's gone too, sucked away on a wave of pain.

With no more reading, I fall even further behind in my least favourite class. And with the infection, I really can't guess at insulin dosage. I have to test four times a day, and my whole right hand feels achy. I test my left fingers—no guitar playing, either.

Overwhelmed and depressed, I drag myself to school on the next Monday, even though I still feel tired and sore. Old Man Veen insists I write his surprise quiz, despite the fact I've been away. I can hear the taunt in his tone; he wants to prove I can't keep up with the rest of the class. He wants me to fail.

I can't give him the satisfaction. I know I would have aced the test had I not been away. When I listen to all my classroom notes on tape, I'm extremely focussed. If anything seems to have improved since I've gone blind, it's that mental focus and, as a result, my memory. I could have blown him away. But I was sick and too depressed to give any attention to my English homework.

Still, there's a way to show him.

With no teaching assistant available, I need to use the only computer in the lab with a screen-reading program. I'm alone with the test—there's no one to supervise.

Will Veen come to check? If he sneaks in on me, I won't see him, after all. I take a chance and log onto the internet looking up all the answers.

When Veen hands the quiz back next day, he makes a big deal about the eighty percent I got. He knows I've cheated; it's all in his smug tone. "No one ever does that well on my tests. I believe Mr. Nicholson is extraordinarily gifted."

He pats my back, and I want to hit his arm away. But I did cheat, and I can't argue with that tone or complain about his condescension.

"And I assume, with your illness, you've had plenty of time to prepare your outline and opening paragraph."

"I have the statement, but not the first paragraph or the body outline."

"Well, you'll lose twenty percent of your mark for that."

Firm but pleasant—again, I can't argue with his tone.

Throughout the class, he calls on me like a sore he's chosen to worry. My brain freezes, and even the answers I know, I can't get out of my mouth fast enough to satisfy him. He flips over to someone else.

His revenge on the cheater.

"If you want to complain to the principal, I'll go with you," Maddie tells me after, as we step into the hall. She strokes my cheek with her hand. It's her smile by touch, nothing more, and I appreciate it.

I grab and squeeze her hand.

"No, thanks. I have to try to work this out on my own."

"Kyle, honestly? Don't—just let it go. You've got to talk to someone about him, otherwise he'll flunk you."

I sigh, knowing she's right. But I cheated, and I have

no right to complain about anything. Twenty percent off my independent study—with that handicap, in fact, Old Man Veen may already have failed me.

Chapter 17

Elizabeth and Magic

Kyle's away a whole week, and I don't hear from him.

"More mind games," Alicia says.

She also tells me whenever she spots Kyle walking with his ex, something I don't really need to hear. Maddie is beautiful, the same age as Kyle is and slightly shorter. They make a great-looking couple, perfect really.

"Do you still want me to read for you?" I finally force myself to confront him on Wednesday.

"Liz, oh yeah. Where've you been? You know I can't look for you."

I tell him what I've seen, but he says Maddie's just a friend and likes to help him out. Too much, he says, which is part of why they broke up.

I accept his answers, about being too sick to call anyone, about his text messaging being down, about him not being sure I wanted to continue with him, all of it—I force myself to believe, because I'm just in too deep to give up.

So—we begin again—to meet over a book. Every day of October, I read after school to Kyle. Nothing else happens. His hand brushes mine, he gives me a kiss when I have to leave. Sometimes I wonder if Alicia's right, if Kyle is only using me. But when our lips do meet, it's like no other sensation I've had—soft and warm yet powerful and consuming. He has to force himself to pull away, like he's holding back for my sake. I'm addicted and can't walk away.

As the book draws to a close, I wonder what will happen to us. The first week of November, we get an early snow, and Kyle startles me with the news that he may be failing English.

"I was sick a week, Liz. Of course, I fell behind." Flushed with frustration, Kyle looks like he needs a break. I know better than to suggest that, though.

"Outline and opening paragraph—gee, Kyle, couldn't you have faked that without reading the whole book?"

I can feel my shoulder blades hard against the wall as we sit together on the floor, me slipping the bookmark between the pages. We only have one chapter to go but it's time for me to leave.

"I could have asked my Mom to help. I wouldn't have told her it was for you. She and Veen used to be buddies in college. She knows how his brain works."

"Never mind your mother helping me, just stay and finish the last chapter," he pleads.

I look at my watch. So what if I'm late for supper, I can tell Mom I was helping a friend with homework.

"Sure," I tell him.

"Can we just shift to the bed, though? I think I'm getting floor sores from sitting here so long."

My shoulder blades and butt bones feel like they're going to burst through my skin so I nod. "Okay."

Beauty is near Kyle's feet, and, as I'm bending my knees to sit, Beauty jumps up on the bed, something I never allowed her to do back when she lived with us.

"Honestly, Beauty, what are you thinking?" Kyle pushes the dog down and slides in beside me.

"She's been acting up a lot lately, hasn't she?" I ask him as I watch Beauty reluctantly touch down on the floor again, ears and tail drooping in disappointment.

"No, she hasn't," he snaps. Beauty skulks under the bed.

"Kyle?" I watch the hardness in his face dissolve. From a straight line, his lips turn first upwards then slightly down. They bunch now, as does the skin around his eyes. Kyle looks scared.

"All right—since I was sick, she's become impossible. I think it was because Shawna had to take her for walks. For all I know, she probably lets Beauty sleep on her bed, too. Now Mom wants to call in the trainer."

"Well, the trainer can suggest things."

"Like I'm the wrong person to have a dog guide? I am, and you've always known I was. You used to say it yourself."

"Come on." I lean towards him and brush his face with my fingers, trying to smooth away his fears. "That was before I got to know you."

He leans forward and our lips touch. I can't pull away. It's as if a tide is washing me towards him. I feel everything inside me loosen and open, even as in the distance I hear a door opening.

"Kyle! What are you doing?" Tall, dark-haired, and slim, the lady standing at the door has to be his mother, the resemblance is so strong. And it seems they share the same lightning-trigger fury.

"You're in bed with a girl. " Her voice snaps like a binder ring.

"Mom, it's not what you think. She's been reading *Blindness* to me. Look, here's the book."

Kyle pats all around on the bed but, of course, the book's still lying on the floor, where we were reading before. I leap up, snatch it, and wave it frantically in front of Mrs. Nicholson's face. Her expression stays granite hard, her features chiselled with anger. Beauty pushes out from under the bed at that moment, too, wagging her tail violently to match the energy in the room. She jumps onto my knees.

"Down, Beauty," I yell at her.

"No wonder the dog doesn't behave. Kyle, I don't care what was happening here. You were told not to see Elizabeth again."

"Well, let's just think about that for a moment, shall we, Mom?" Kyle's voice sounds dry with a bitterness I haven't heard before. "I've never seen Elizabeth in my entire life."

His mother's face flushes a deep crimson as she steps towards him, sputtering.

"I'll be going home now," I interrupt. "Kyle, maybe your mother can finish the last chapter for you."

Kyle stands up from the bed now.

"Wait for me. I'll walk you home." He rushes out after me. His mother stays in the bedroom, counting to a hundred—or whatever else she does to calm down.

At the front door, Beauty horses around before stepping into the harness. Once again, I'm astounded at her bad behaviour. Too much unchannelled energy.

Kyle and I struggle into our coats as Beauty circles and tangles herself between us.

"Beauty, forward!" Kyle finally commands and we head outside.

"This probably isn't the best idea. You'll have to walk the whole way back yourself." The wind howls cold around us. Pumped with anger, Kyle really power marches. We're past the bus stop by the time he answers me.

"I don't know, Liz. I want to be with you as much as possible. Every time we're together feels like the last time."

I squeeze his arm. I know how he feels, and since his Mom caught us, who know what will happen? We huddle together against the wind, me hanging back so that Beauty can lead.

At the park, I spot a small figure throwing stones into the river. The figure looks lonelier and sadder than I feel. "Oh, my gosh, it's Donald. Doesn't he ever go home?"

"Maybe he forgot his key again. He should tie it around his neck." Kyle shakes his head. "Kid wants to be a lawyer when he grows up. He'd better train his memory a little better."

I chuckle. "Oh, Kyle. Donald doesn't really want to be lawyer. You told him you want to study law. Donald wants to be exactly like you."

I spot his backpack on a bench. Donald hasn't even gone home from school yet. I shake my head.

"He worships you, Kyle. Do you know he dresses just like you and fixes his hair exactly like yours?'

"You're kidding." Kyles sounds amazed but pleased. A smile creeps across his face. "I always thought he just hung around me because of Beauty."

"And he wants a dog just like you, too. All he ever talks about is the dog his mother says she'll get him."

"Okay, so I'll be nicer to him," Kyle says and stops for a moment.

"I'm not exactly the greatest role model. Tell me something..." He pauses and his mouth buckles with emotion. "Do you think I could ever make a good dad?"

I stare back at him for a moment. Guys don't ask stuff like that—for sure Scott never does. He hates babies, especially when they're crying. Certainly, he never thinks about having a family of his own. But Kyle's asking something more, I think—it's like he's wondering whether he can ever have a normal, everyday kind of life. I smile, remembering Kyle holding and rocking Teal, singing to him.

"Of course, you will," I answer.

CHAPTER 18

Kyle Alone

Mom gets the last laugh on me for sneaking Liz over behind her back. She calls Canine Vision to report Beauty's bad behaviour. The trainer comes and, watching Beauty act up, especially around Shawna, insists she goes back for remedial training. I'm totally helpless and dependent again. The next week, I kick my locker in frustration at the end of the school day. Did I just spin the wrong combination, or did I miscount lockers?

"I can't stand it," I complain to Ryan. At least I hope it's Ryan, still standing there.

"How did I ever get along without Beauty? Everybody keeps asking about her, too. Someone started the rumour that I'd shaken her to death."

"Who cares?" He slaps my shoulder. "Tomorrow's Friday. Lighten up. Next week, you'll get your doggie back, right?"

Bang. Ryan shuts his locker and his mind to my problems. "Like you said, you got along without her before."

"Uh huh. Remember how you ditched me in the mall bathroom that lunch hour?"

"Can't say I do, my man. I swear you are gifted with memory. See ya around."

"Wait!" I reach out and grab some part of his jacket.

"Yeah, what?"

"You promised to take me to the library." The library is where I've been meeting Liz since Mom found us in my room. Liz finished reading *Blindness* to me, and we worked on the essay in the computer lab.

"Right! Come this way."

I grab hold of his arm and shuffle alongside him. It's humiliating. This is a school I've gone to for four years, and I still can't make my own way to the library. Depending on Mr. Undependable again—that's humiliating, too.

As we step into the library, a horrible thought forms, even as Elizabeth calls for me to come and sit next to her by the computer. What if Beauty doesn't shape up during the week away? I trip over a few chairs and finally stumble into the empty one beside her. The thought turns into a clear hard bubble that I recognize. They won't give her back to me then, and I won't be able to go to Queens like this—not by myself.

Liz's baby-sweet scent melts me, and her voice talking

about my essay plays a song through my whole body. But I can feel my throat seize up. Liz won't go with me to Queen's next year. She's not old enough. I need Beauty.

Mom ranted about a lot of things that day when she caught us "*in bed together*," as she put it—how Liz was too young for me; how her mother hated me and how I could never turn that around; how there were lots of other girls perfect for me—what about Maddison, for heaven's sake? But the only thing she said that made any sense was this: Beauty would never entirely be my dog as long as her previous foster owner, Elizabeth, was around me.

"Liz, stop reading the essay for a moment. Tell me what you look like."

"Do you want to feel my face and see for yourself?"

I smile. It's a common misconception among sighted people. They think somehow I can magically piece together their appearance by running my hands over their eyes, noses, and mouths. But with Liz, for this one last time, I do want to touch her.

"Yeah, but tell me, too. I want to try to form a picture in my mind." I hear her sigh as she lifts my hands and puts them on her face.

I move them back over her head. "I know your hair is red, but what shade is it exactly? Carrot-coloured?"

"No. You're going to laugh, but it's almost the same colour as Beauty's, maybe one shade brighter."

My fingers bump over thick curls. "That doesn't help me much. I've never seen Beauty, either." I tangle my fingers in what feels like ringlets.

"Okay, how about this: Do you remember the colour of fall leaves once they land on the ground?"

I nod.

"That's about the same colour as my hair."

"Mmm."

"It gets frizzy. But when I iron it, the stupid curls flatten and my hair goes smooth."

I move my fingers to her forehead and run them over her eyebrows down onto her eyelids.

"My eyebrows are lighter, and my eyelashes, well, they're white—except I'm wearing mascara today."

"Your skin, what colour is it?" It feels smooth and warm beneath my fingers.

"White, I don't tan well. And pink—I blush easily. I guess my skin is pretty pale. But I have freckles across my nose."

"Freckles," I repeat. Maddie has freckles too, I remember; I try to imagine a curly-haired girl with autumn-coloured hair and a sunshine-kissed nose. "What colour are your eyes?"

"Light brown, with darker flecks surrounding the pupils. It's almost like I have freckles in my eyes."

My fingers slide over her cheeks.

"I have a round face and apple cheeks. The freckles

and the cheeks make me look young."

Ryan's big problem with her. But it's not mine. For me, the only problem is Beauty. My thumbs brush over Liz's lips. They're soft and moist, and I don't resist kissing them. For one moment, I forget about Beauty, too. All I care about is this.

Then we break apart again. Liz clears her throat. I remember the big problem between us, and my face turns warm.

"Listen..." I pause and drop my voice lower. "There's something else we have to talk about." I stop for a moment and inhale deeply. My chest tightens anyway. The bottom of my throat closes up.

"Kyle?" Liz sounds young and hurt, and already so far away. "I'm not going to like this, am I?"

I shake my head. "Neither of us will. You know I have to go away to school next year."

"You don't have to; you said you could go to Mac. That's not even a half hour away."

"But I want to go Queens. I need to get away from my mother.... I have to make it on my own." My voice breaks and Elizabeth slips her hand in mine. I swallow and start again.

"Your mother won't even let us go out anyway. I can live with the sneaking around. I can do that for you. You're worth it. But..." She kisses my hand, and I pull it away. "But I can't live without Beauty."

"You'll have her back on Monday. Didn't the trainer say she was doing well?" Liz rushes the words out at once.

"The trainer said Beauty will never listen to me with you around. You know that yourself. We have to break up."

Liz's voice dissolves into soft kitten sobs. It's the most beautiful sound in the world, what I fell in love with really, that first day, when she tripped over the grate at Little Stone Park. She quietly cries out all the feelings that I can't really show to anyone.

I want to hold her and feel her shoulders shake. I reach my hands out, but pull them back. It will only make things worse, when I can't let go. "I'll always love you, you know that."

I touch her shoulder lightly and then stumble away.

Chapter 19

Elizabeth and Magic

An hour in the library, and then I take the long way home, crying all the way. It's already dark outside and has to be one of the coldest November days on record. My tears feel as though they're beading into ice on my cheeks. My nose feels like it's fallen off my face. It's pretty late when I finally turn onto our walkway. Mom's car sits in the driveway, ticking the way it does when the engine's just been shut off, but it sounds as impatient as Mom can be. I step through the door, expecting the worst.

"I thought you said she was walking Magic. Why is the dog still in her crate?" Mom keeps talking at Rolph, as if I haven't just walked in and am standing right beside her. She's still dressed in her teacher dress—pants and jacket—so she must have beaten me home by minutes.

Yeah, stupid! I look at Rolph. If he didn't always keep Magic crated, Mom wouldn't have even noticed. Rolph opens his eyes wide at me, in panic.

"Sorry, what a brain!" He slaps the heel of his hand against his forehead. "You were going to see Alicia, right?" There's a knifelike sharpness in his eyes. *We're in this together*, it says.

I feel sick. I'm stuck, even though I don't want to be in with Rolph on anything.

Anyway, if Mom looks my way she'll be able to read the lie from my face, no doubt red and smudged from the crying and the cold. I turn to the crate to hide, and to let Magic out.

But Mom's not paying any attention to me, anyway. Teal's just finished a crawl to Magic's food dishes, and now he slaps his hand on the water in one of the dishes, splashing it everywhere. "Don't, baby!" she calls.

"Teal, don't," Rolph repeats, and rushes to scoop the baby up.

"I caught him eating dog food from the cupboard earlier." Rolph clicks his tongue at Magic—as though it's her fault. "Do you think he's all right?"

I give Rolph a look. He's dressed in a grease-stained grey sweatsuit. Slob. Doesn't he ever watch Teal when he's around? I'd like to tell him exactly what I think of him but remember the expression in his eyes, knife blades shining, so I grit my teeth. Instead, I just kneel beside Magic and pat her.

"We'll have to put the kibble up higher." Mom wipes up the water with a rag. "Don't worry. He'll be fine. All kids try pet food at some time or another."

Mom's so busy with Teal, she doesn't have time to consider that Rolph's explanation about where I was makes no sense—Magic would have come with me to Alicia's. Her constant preoccupation is useful lately. She has no clue about Kyle. Not that it matters, when it's all over between us. I can't believe it's over.

The phone rings. Kyle? He has to change his mind.

Mom leans over to check call-display.

"It's Alicia. Honestly, Elizabeth, you just left her. What could you possibly have to say to each other already?"

"Shakespeare homework."

Only half a lie, since I really need to work on my own project for a change. I quickly scoop up the portable. "Let's go, Magic." She follows me to my room and watches me talk to Alicia.

"You nearly blew my cover calling just now," I tell her, "but am I ever glad to hear your voice." I slump back on my bed, and Magic leaps up beside me. Then I unload about everything that happened in the library.

Alicia stays pretty quiet.

"You're not saying anything. What do you think?"

"Well, what do you want me to say? It was inevitable. Your mother would have found out about you seeing him sooner or later. And, like he said, he is going away in September."

"But there's a lot of time left—and other people have long-distance relationships."

"In Hollywood, where everyone has tons of money and chases after each other on last-minute flights. But not people like us, who rely on our parents to pay our long-distance bills."

"Still, that's in September, next year. It's not even Christmas yet."

"You're not going to like this."

"Try me."

"He finished his essay. He doesn't need you."

"He wasn't using me!"

"Don't be mad! You made me tell you. This is what always happens. Guys get in the way!" Alicia sighs.

"I love him," I whisper.

"Oh, Liz." She hears I'm crying now. "In case you haven't noticed, he's blind. That's going to be a pretty big disadvantage later."

"It doesn't matter to me." My voice breaks.

She sighs again. "Okay. Stop crying then. It's worth another try." She waits a breath for me and then continues. "You know dogs. Remember when Beauty used to be spooked by buses? You trained the fear out of her using treats and a tape recorder. Convince Kyle you can find a way to make Beauty behave for him, too."

Hmm—she'd hit on something, something tucked way at the back of my mind about Beauty. With Kyle, the dog seemed overcharged with energy, like a grade-school kid who'd suffered too many indoor recesses. When I threw the stick at the park for Magic, I remembered playing with Beauty in just that way. Did Kyle ever throw the stick for her? His sister Shawna used to throw the ball for Beauty. Maybe Beauty needed more exercise and more playing time with Kyle. And what if Beauty saw more of me paired up with Magic? Hard as it was for her, wouldn't she finally realize that she no longer belonged to me?

"You're brilliant!" I tell Alicia over the phone as I look down at Magic. She wags her tail in agreement. When I smile, she throws one golden paw on my knee and lifts her ears as if hoping for more good news. "I'll show Kyle how to make Beauty listen to him."

"Great, I'm glad I could solve your problem for you. But I called for another reason. Friday night, Scott wants me to go to his uncle's ski chalet with him. Can you cover for me?"

"You're going someplace overnight with Scott?"

"Don't say it like that. We aren't going to do anything. It's just too far to drive back in one day, and we want to get some early morning skiing in."

"You don't ski." Stupid comment. Alicia goes along with anything her boyfriends do. Rollerblading, skiing, watching hours of sports.

She doesn't even pretend to disagree with me.

"So what's your point, really? Listen, you cover for me Friday, and if you get back together with Kyle, I'll cover for you sometime."

There's a bad taste in my mouth suddenly, like kibble-breath—Magic breathing on me? Her head rests heavily on my knee. I pat her head—no, nothing to do with her breath. If I lie for Alicia, she'll lie for me—just like what I'm doing with Rolph. Neither feels right. Still, what would it be like to go on a regular date with Kyle, no reading or essay writing involved? If I can convince him about Beauty and get him back, I'll have Alicia's favour in my back pocket, like a plane ticket, waiting.

"Okay, sure. Gotta go now. I have to work on that Shakespeare essay."

"See you tomorrow." A breezy, light goodbye for her—for me, it feels like something important has ended with the click of that receiver. Truth and honour? Innocence? I stare at the phone for a few seconds and shake my head—that all ended a long time ago, when Mom forbade me to see Kyle.

"Let's go downstairs, Magic. We've got an essay to tackle."

She wags her tail and springs to her feet. A walk anywhere is exciting to her. She races me down the stairs, and when I'm seated at the computer, she lies down on my feet. I search the net for some opinions on Shylock. I swear the research takes me twice as long as writing the thing. And all the time, I'm thinking over what Alicia said. If I convince Kyle about Beauty, she'll cover for me so we can go out. Stupid Ryan has a party every weekend. What if I just show up at one? Would Kyle be there? Too risky. I swallow hard and message him.

Red: I think I know how 2 make sure Beauty listens to u. I press *Send*, and my fingers hover over the keys, waiting and hoping Kyle's online. Ding! Hurray, he's there.

Music Man: I'm willing to try anything.

I type back, *Are u really?*

Music Man: It's like I'm dead without you.

I smile, because I believe him. Alicia's wrong, Kyle could never just use me. I type again.

Red: When's Ryan's next party? Alicia says she'll cover for me.

Music Man: Saturday, I'll be there early.

Red: Okay, I'll find a way to be there too. I sign off just as another Ding signals—Alicia wants to message.

Playgirl: Liz, u r home Friday, right? Make sure u take any phone calls from my mother.

Red: I said I'd cover for u, didn't I?

Playgirl: U r a true friend.

Red: No problem. U need to cover for me Saturday night. I'm going to Ryan's party to be with Kyle.

Playgirl: My idea worked. Cool!

Suddenly, I feel a hand on my shoulder and quickly snap the window shut.

"Sorry, Liz. Did I interrupt?" It's Dad, and he's carrying a My Computers bag.

"Look at this. George got me this prototype webcam. Check it out. One setting gives you wide-angle motion sensor recording—it's a complete security system. The other one will just let your friends see you when you message them."

"That's great." I smile for a second, thinking how I can use that to stay in touch with Kyle next year. Then I realize it won't do Kyle any good.

"Just give me a second, Dad, then you can have the computer all to yourself to hook it up."

"Sure, honey." Dad leaves the little round camera on the desk and heads back upstairs.

I open the window up again and type.

Red: Dad's going 2 b installing a webcam for the next little while don't type anything personal.

I sign off.

"Dad, you can have it now!" I call.

"Back upstairs, girl," I tell Magic as I stand. Magic races me for the stairs and beats me to the top. I open the door for her, and she scrambles ahead—only to knock into Rolph.

I see him lift his leg to kick her away. It's a quick, nasty move that matches the look on his face.

Magic makes a quick move of her own. It's half a lunge, with half a growl.

Rolph leaps back now. "Did you see that? That dog is vicious."

Dad walks in at that moment. "Liz, did Magic just snap at Rolph?" he asks.

"No, well yes. But Rolph kicked her."

"I did not. I merely pushed the dog away with my foot. This animal isn't safe around Teal. I've been talking to Debra about this, believe me."

"Talking about Magic?" I scrunch up my eyes at him. "Magic is perfectly safe. If Magic had really wanted to bite you, you wouldn't have a foot left."

It isn't really the right thing to say to reassure him—he looks even more afraid of the dog now. But I'm afraid, too. What has he suggested to my sister as a solution, seeing he thinks Magic too vicious to be around Teal?

Chapter 20

Kyle Alone

"I only took one extra week. You can deduct marks. I realize that. I'm not asking for special favours."

Friday morning, before the bell rings, Maddie waits at the door for me as I hold out my essay to Mr. Veen.

He does not take it from my hands. No sympathetic noises come from him either—I sense that he's a brick wall. No sounds come from him at all, till he clears his throat, and then his *ahem* sounds antagonistic.

"You didn't submit any of your opening lines or supporting statements on the due dates." A blast of poison wind from him—he must know about me surfing the net for the pop quiz. Now he thinks I'm cheating again. Still…

"But I can't write like that. And I've done all the work, what does it matter?"

"I'm sure you've done all the work," he answers.

I shake my head. I'm right; he's pegged me for a

cheater. "If I hired someone to write the essay, wouldn't they make sure to deliver it on time?"

"I don't know, and I don't care."

"But I need a good English grade to get into Queens."

"Oh, really. I'm sure they'll make special allowances to let you in. They must have some quota."

"What is your problem, exactly?" Maddie's voice suddenly calls out from right beside me. "Why won't you just look at his paper and grade it? He's not asking for any special favours."

"Oh, isn't he? I'm not stupid. I checked the computer you wrote the quiz on, Kyle. The history of the Internet sites used, in particular."

Bang. My face gets red. I know what is coming.

"I can't prove that it was you who logged on those sites that day, but you and I both know you did."

"We're talking about this paper," I tell him. "And I wrote it myself." But isn't that partly a lie, too? Liz read the book to me and typed all my thoughts out for me.

"Come on, let's go." Madison tugs my elbow. "We can get someone else to grade it."

For a moment, I still hold out the essay, but then I turn, grab onto Maddie's arm and follow her out the door.

"Someone else? Do you think any of the teachers in this school will second-guess Mr. Veen?"

"I don't know. We have to try."

"But, Maddie...it's true. I surfed the net to answer his pop quiz."

Maddie sighs. "So what? Did you write that essay or not?"

"You know I did. I worked really hard on it."

"Well, then, come on, Kyle. You want to be a lawyer, don't you? You know you're innocent till proven guilty. You just have to fight him on this."

I smile, grateful she isn't chewing me out about the quiz. "Yeah, I guess you're right. But for now, Maddie, I just want to make it to my French class so I can turn in that book report. Can you get me there in time?"

Maddie guides me to my class swiftly, as she has been doing the whole week. This is the last day. Beauty will return Monday, a school holiday, so I can spend the whole day with her. Just as Liz suggested, I'm going to spend more time playing with Beauty. I can hardly wait. I've missed her so much.

I put Veen out of my mind. Tomorrow's the party, and I'm going with Elizabeth. It's good that Beauty won't be around. Nothing to get between Elizabeth and me, no essays to write and no misbehaving dog.

Saturday afternoon, Ryan comes by early—so that I can do the white cane trick to get beer for the party. Without Beauty, that takes forever, too. People like to approach a dog; they don't want to step forward to a beggar. Together we pick up Elizabeth from Alicia's house, Ryan's exchange for the humiliating beer run. She's hanging out there for her parents' sake.

"Gosh, I wish you'd come earlier," Liz says as I step out of the front of the Mustang so she can slide in the back. "Alicia's mom started to get chatting with us, and I nearly slipped up about Alicia and Scott's little trip out of the city."

"I wish I'd been here sooner, too." I touch her arm to draw her closer. "Sorry."

I kiss her so long that Ryan gives us a whistle.

"Did you hand in your essay?" Liz asks as she gets in the back. "What a relief to get that out of the way."

"Would be, except Old Man Veen won't accept it now. I'm going to have to get someone else to mark it and stand up to him."

"My mom would look at it. She can convince him, too, if only she doesn't know it's yours. We'll give her a blind copy, and I'll just tell her it's my friend's."

"Blind copy...that's good!" Ryan chuckles. "What are you going to do? Take the ink cartridge out when you print the sucker?"

"Oh, honestly, give it up, Ryan. I'll just give her a copy with no name on it," Liz says.

I don't feel entirely safe with that idea. As soon as they talk, Veen will realize whose paper it is. But for now, I don't argue. We're going to have a good time at a party together, which is a first. So far, all we've ever done together is homework—and Rollerblading that one time.

When we get to Ryan's party, Liz and I both take a beer, just to carry around and fit in with the rest of the crowd. Liz sips at it but complains about the taste. We sit on the couch together, then someone hands me his guitar. To be the performer felt good when I partied solo, but now, I just want to spend time with Liz. So I beg off after a couple songs and dance a slow number with her.

It's the best thing that's happened to me all week. Her sweet baby-powder smell floats all around me, and I float, too. She sways against me, her hair tickling up against my chin. Autumn hair, I remember her telling me. Freckled eyes, freckled nose—a picture of her forms in mind. She is beautiful and I hold her closer.

She lifts her head and kisses me—soft, soft lips. Everything with Liz is sweet and gentle and makes my skin burn for more. We linger together for beat after beat of music, till Ryan jeers again. "My bedroom's around the corner."

"Come on, Liz," I whisper. "Let's take him up on that."

"I don't know. I'd feel funny," she answers.

"We can be alone and talk without anyone bothering us. Otherwise they'll make me sing again." I take her hand, and she leads where I tell her to go, back towards Ryan's room. We shove the coats off the bed so we can sit there side by side, backs against the wall. We talk more about how we should handle Beauty when she gets back. Liz will bring Magic, and we can both play with our dogs at the same time. Beauty will learn that I'm the only one for her. It's something the trainer explained to me and Liz repeats, "You need to be the one who does everything for and with Beauty."

"If only that would work—I've got to try, Liz. I don't know if I can live without you." I kiss her again, and she moans.

Then she pulls away. "I...I can't."

"Do you want to watch some television?" I ask. We've never had the chance to do ordinary things together.

"You like TV?" she asks me.

"Sure, what time is it anyway?" I push the button on my talking watch. "Eleven o'clock," a deep voice answers. I tell Liz about my favourite comedy show, which is on right now, descriptive view.

"Descriptive...oh you mean, someone tells you what's happening on the screen?"

"Yeah. Do you see the remote somewhere?"

I hear the set come on and tell her how to get the DV option. Meanwhile, I tuck my arm around her waist. It feels like heaven—we're together, nothing else to think about for a change.

On TV, the comic draws a big audience laugh, but it feels like they're laughing at us, with us. Liz chuckles too, like a stream bubbling. I smile and lean my head on her shoulder. I could stay this way forever—everything and everyone else so far away.

Suddenly, the door bangs open.

"Phone for you, Elizabeth. Better get downstairs." Ryan's voice. "Your mom knows where you are, and she's on her way over."

Chapter 21

Elizabeth Alone

"Liz, I'm sorry." Alicia's on the other end of the phone. "Your mother just showed up here and insisted on speaking to you, some kind of emergency. I had to tell her where you were."

"What time did she show up?" I ask, as if that will make any difference. The doorbell rings before she can even answer. "Never mind. Gotta go."

"Call me!" she commands as I disconnect and hand Ryan back the phone. He takes it and opens the door.

Mom stands there, shoulders hunched in her fun-fur coat, mouth puckered tightly shut, eyes squinting. It's freezing out, which is why her breath comes out in smoke clouds. She looks like some kind of fire-breathing polyester bear.

"I'll get my jacket." I slam the door on her and push through the crowds of kids, huddled in the hall smoking and drinking. When I get back to the room, I paw through the pile of coats at the foot of the bed.

"Elizabeth?" Kyle calls to me.

"My mother's here. Don't come out. It will only make things worse."

I dash back, slip out quickly, so Mom can't see too much of the party scene. My mother walks ahead of me silently to the car. She opens the door and slides in.

"You smell of beer," she finally says as she turns on the ignition. I'm only half in the car, so I rush to get my side shut and buckle my seatbelt.

"You lied to me; you know you weren't supposed to be at this party." She half turns to check behind us, puts the van into reverse and backs out of the driveway.

"I've been seeing Kyle," I tell her quietly as she shifts into drive.

"Pardon?" Her eyes never leave the road. It's much easier talking to her this way.

"After school, I've been helping him with his homework. I went to this party to be with him. That's why I lied."

"I trusted you!"

"No, you didn't—or you wouldn't have forbidden me to see him."

"You'll be grounded forever."

"If you won't let me see him, I don't care anyway." We drive by the park, and I can see the river by the bridge has frozen almost completely over. I shiver and wipe tears from my face.

Mom puts her hand on mine for a second.

"Look, we'll have to talk about all this later. Rolph and Deb are at the hospital with Teal. Magic bit him."

"What? Is Teal all right?"

"Oh, he's fine. But he does have teeth marks on his arm and broken skin."

"Oh, Mom, Magic would never bite Teal. More likely they're Rolph's teeth marks."

Mom actually smiles, then shakes her head.

"I don't know. Rolph was alone with them at the time, and when I came home he had Teal all bundled up to go. He says either we get rid of Magic, or Teal should live with him."

"Can he do that?" I ask.

Mom shrugs her shoulders. "People seem to do whatever they want these days."

We roll into the driveway, and I jump out of the car. I just have to see Magic. I almost expect her to have transformed into some rabies-crazed beast, drooling white foam, but it's still loveable old Magic who comes to the door and throws her paws over my shoulder when I bend down to her.

"She can't have bitten Teal; you know that, Mom."

Mom shrugs her shoulders as she hangs up her coat. We head into the kitchen where Dad sits waiting. He repeats all the stuff about the teeth marks, but I just shake my head.

"Liz, I've seen that dog with Rolph. She's snapped at him a couple of times."

"So has everyone! Rolph never takes care of Teal. He sleeps on the couch and lets him wander and get into everything."

My parents look unconvinced. "He still drinks, too."

My father winces, then takes a breath. "Alcoholic or not, he can't have imagined the marks, Liz. We've already called Canine Vision. We're taking her back on Monday."

"Oh my god! What will they do to her? They won't use her to breed if they think she's aggressive."

My father looks towards my mother, who doesn't say anything, just shrugs her shoulders.

That's when it hits me. They'll put Magic down. Nobody has any use for a dog that bites.

"You can't let them take her!" I tell them and hug Magic so hard she yelps. "I'm sorry, girl."

I loosen my arms and turn towards Dad. "Did you see that? I choked her, but she didn't snap or growl. Rolph's got to be lying." Magic woofs, as if to agree, but then I hear car doors slamming and realize she's announcing someone's arrival.

"That'll be Rolph and Debra back from the hospital now," Dad says.

Debra walks in with Teal, who's gurgling and happy.

He's wearing a blue and red snowsuit with a matching court-jester hat that jingles.

"He's fine. No need for a fuss." Debra hands him to Rolph as she throws her duffle coat over a hook.

"This time, he's fine." Rolph looks rumpled again—doesn't he ever shave anymore? His down-filled vest probably cost a bundle, but without the sleeves it can't be keeping him warm in this weather; and the way it puffs out his chest makes him look ridiculous.

I want to throw something at him. "They're going to kill Magic because of you."

"What? I'm not telling them what to do with that animal. I just refuse to subject my son to its moods. I have plenty of room in my apartment. Teal can live with me."

I see the look Debra gives him and understand something else is going on, though what, I don't know. I see the expression on his face—he seems satisfied, maybe even happy, about the evening's events.

"Come on, Magic." I double slap the top of my leg. "You can sleep in my room tonight. You'll be safe there."

We both take off into my room, escaping any more lectures. As fast as the tears fall down my face, Magic licks them off. I think angry little-kid thoughts for a while, about how we should run away. Then Magic would be safe, and they'd all be sorry. But it's no good. I'm adult enough now to know I couldn't make it work. Where could I stay with a dog; how could I feed her?

But I can't sleep, either. I toss and turn, and wish it were a decent hour so I could call Alicia and tell her how awful my life has turned in one day. My eyes feel gritty and heavy, but I'm all charged up with energy that doesn't know where to go. Finally, at five o'clock in the morning, I decide to sneak downstairs and e-mail Alicia. Who knows, she might be online, too, and then we can message each other.

Stumbling over a stuffed hippopotamus at the bottom of the stairs, I make my way to the computer. I nearly trip again over the iron. Then I slump down on the plastic garden chair in front of the computer. I sigh and stare at the computer screen while the e-mail program opens. I click on the new message. How do I even begin to describe what may happen to Magic? It's too depressing to put in words.

I swallow hard and stare off into space. That's when I notice the little round lens of the webcam. Is it supposed to be on the desk like that? I thought Dad clipped it to the screen. It's like an alien, watching me. Is that red light supposed to be on? Someone must have been fooling with it. Oh my gosh, the security button's activated.

Idly, I push the hot key to see what the thing's been recording. I see Teal's face large, his features distorted. Teal must have fooled around with it. That would prove that he's completely unsupervised when Rolph rolls up on the couch for his nap.

I watch as Teal takes his wobbly two-step from the computer desk to the ironing board. I didn't leave that out yesterday, did I? Teal stumbles and grabs the cord of the iron.

Golden fur fills the picture now, and in the last fuzzy image, Magic grabs Teal by the arm and yanks him out of the way of the iron. I look behind me to where the ironing board still stands. The iron is lying on its side on the floor.

Magic is a hero, and Rolph would let her be destroyed for it.

I rush to Debra's room and pound on her door. "Deb, come here, you have to come see this."

"What, what?" She opens the door to her room. "Is Teal crying?"

"No, Deb. You have to come see what the webcam recorded."

She rubs her eyes and sighs. "Liz, honestly. Do you have any idea how little sleep I get since Teal was born?"

"But they're taking Magic away today—and she's innocent."

"Fine, let's see what couldn't wait till a decent hour."

She slips on a bathrobe and hugs it closely around her as she follows me to the computer.

I sit at the keyboard and replay the scene where Magic rescues Teal. Debra stares at it and says nothing.

"Whenever Rolph looks after Teal, he just switches on the television and falls asleep," I explain. "I told him to at least let Magic out of her crate so she could look after him—and she did!"

Another heavy sigh. "I know Rolph is not perfect."

"Not perfect, he's a liar. He still drinks, too; do you know that?"

"I do indeed."

I turn and squint at her, not understanding. Why wouldn't she just get rid of this jerk?

"You only want to see the bad in him, Liz. Rolph really thinks Magic is dangerous. That's the truth, as he sees it."

"Deb, Rolph is dangerous. He can't be around Teal."

"Rolph is his father, and no matter what, Teal has a right to have access to his dad. That's what the lawyer told me."

"You talked to a lawyer?" I ask her quietly.

"Yes, and I know what you're thinking. But listen to me: Rolph wants us to try living together as a family again."

"You can't, Deb. He's just going to hit you again."

"He never hit me, Liz." She stares back into my eyes, unblinking.

"Oh, come on. That lame story about him opening the door into your face."

"He was drunk, and it was an accident," Debra tells me.

"You can't go."

"I have to. Liz, I love him. I always have. I think we can work things out. He has a contract here in Canada again. There won't be so much pressure on him. And if we don't live together, Teal will have to go alone to him on weekends and for overnight visits during the week."

"That's what the lawyer said?"

Debra nods.

"Maybe we should show him the webcam recording."

"It won't make a difference to our plans. I've made up my mind."

"So you're leaving and taking Teal with you?"

I can't breathe, my chest hurts so much. All the times that kid ruined my life, and now, when I'll be totally free, it feels like something is cracking up inside me.

"But we're staying right here in Oakville. It won't be like before. You can always come to visit us."

"Sure. It will be just perfect." I'm not going to cry. I won't let myself. I might never stop. "Have you told Mom?"

Deb shakes her head.

Funny, how neither of us worry about how Dad will take something. And he's the one who renovated the basement so that Deb and Teal would have bedrooms. I buckle my mouth and think.

"I've still got to tell them about the ironing board thing. Otherwise Canine Vision may put Magic down."

"Of course you do. Honestly, Liz. Rolph couldn't have known about that."

I look at the upturned iron. "You're right, he probably slept through the whole thing. Otherwise he would have cleaned up the evidence." Then I think a selfish thought. "You're going to tell them today, I mean, about moving out?"

"Yup."

That meant everyone would be upset and annoyed at Debra and Rolph. My partying at the Comatose Palace would be forgotten.

A ding from the computer signals someone's messaging me.

Playgirl: If you're there, call me Liz. We have to talk.

Debra sees the message.

"You go ahead and call her; I'm going to try for some more sleep."

I pick up the downstairs phone and get Alicia first ring. I tell her everything about Magic and Teal, ending with how Debra will move back in with Rolph anyway. Just like our last phone call, Alicia doesn't interrupt once. Odd–I almost think the phone is dead.

"You there?" I ask.

"Uh huh." She still doesn't say anything, and I can't help wondering why not.

"Is something wrong?" I finally ask.

"Yes." I hear her crying at the other end.

"Alicia, tell me. What's the matter?"

"Scott and I...Scott and I..."

I squeeze my eyes shut, and hope I'm not going to hear what I know she's going to say.

"Scott and I broke up. He's gone back to Gwen again."

Chapter 22

Kyle Alone

Waking up in my bed with a stale, yeasty taste in my mouth and a pounding in my head, I realize we never should have gone to the Comatose Palace last night. For Liz and me, everything was wrong there. All those kids drinking—it's not like that's what I want to do.

Not when I'm happy anyway. But after her mother took her away, I chugged away at a beer.

"I can't believe it. I don't have my girlfriend or my dog," I remember saying to some girl beside me as I took a swig from the bottle. I felt her squeezing my arm in sympathy, leaning onto my shoulder. Even through that beery haze, I knew I'd be screwing up my blood sugar. I remember singing on the way home, and then a pitch-black void, which I'll call sleep, because I woke up from it right here in my own bed this morning.

Ding-dong! Ding-dong! A doorbell and some voices.

Shoot—what time is it? I press the button on my wrist-watch. "The time is now 11:00."

Maddie's talking to Mom. Mom calls out to me.

Oh, my gosh, why is she here? I scramble up and holler for her to give me ten minutes. I get to the bathroom, wash up quickly, brush my teeth, and then gargle, hoping to get rid of the coating left on my tongue. Back in my room, I change into some different clothes and stuff the smelly beery ones under the bed. Then I reach for a needle on my bureau to test my blood. There's a knock on my door now.

"Come in, ow, damn."

"Your mother gave me a tray of breakfast for you. She said you should have eaten hours ago," Maddie tells me.

"Do you need help with that?"

"What? I can manage."

"Let me," she says softly. "I know how awful it is if you have to retest. Let me just put this tray down on your desk. There." Her voice is near now, and she holds my finger closer to the glucometer. With her help, the blood lands right on target. She's not squeamish about it. For her, it's just good practice for when she studies medicine.

"Sorry. Not ready for company. I had a late night."

"So I gathered," she says and then clicks her tongue when she hears the blood reading. "You drank, too."

I slip the pen under my shirt and inject a higher dose than usual.

"I'm stupid, Maddie. I do some really stupid things."

"Don't we all." Regret in her voice, after all this time.

"Listen, your mother called me. She was worried about you—thinks you're going to run yourself down again. Wanted me to come and visit. Are you okay?"

"I'm fine. My mother just wants us to go out again. She likes you."

"And what about you, Kyle?" Maddie asks.

I inhale deeply. Her cologne, Tangerine Sunrise, mingles with the smell of bacon and eggs. "I really love Liz."

"I thought so."

She's quiet awhile, and for once I'm glad I can't see someone's face.

"Is there any breakfast for you on the tray?" I ask.

"No, I ate earlier. You eat. While I'm here, do you have all the rough work for your essay somewhere on a disk?"

"Yeah, sure. None of that opening line and supporting statement stuff Veen wants. But we finished the paper at school, so it's all on that disk in my backpack."

I sit on the bed, letting Maddie have the chair at the desk.

"Your eggs are at twelve o'clock, there's some bacon at three o'clock, and one toast at nine. I'm switching Perfect Paul off. I can't think when he reads out loud."

"Me neither, unfortunately," I say as I pick up my

toast. I wonder about Elizabeth. What did her mother say when she caught her at the party? How did she even find out? I can't even call her to talk about it.

"Okay, this is all good stuff," Maddie says. "You have a few rougher versions of the piece, there's some brainstorming here. I'll print it all off as supporting documents to hand in with your essay."

"Would you print off another copy of the essay for me, too? Take the name off the header. I may give it to Elizabeth for her mother to read. She's a college English teacher."

"And you need to take the name off because...?"

I have to explain how Liz isn't allowed to see me.

"Too bad. I think mothers would really like you, if they gave you a chance." I hear the smile in her voice. Maddie's mom never liked her seeing "such an unhealthy boy," as she put it.

Is Maddie right, though? Is there some way I can get Mrs. Kerr to give me a chance, to let me go out with Liz without going behind her back?

Monday morning, Mom drives me to pick up Beauty, and I can't believe how happy I feel again. The dog slaps me to death with her tail and lathers my face with her tongue. I don't cringe. I put my arm around her and lean into her fur.

"It will be different, girl, this time. I promise it will be different."

And I start right away. It's freezing outside, but I cover my hands and ears, and I take her for a walk. Mom bought me a special dog toy to throw in the park, and that's where I take Beauty. I take her out of her harness and throw the hunk of hard rubber. Now I have to trust her to run back to me. I inhale deeply, feeling my nose hairs clump together with the frost. It's the longest wait in the world–and then I feel her muzzle at my knee.

"Beauty. Good girl!" I shout. "Great girl. You're amazing." I take the toy and throw it out far again.

Seconds later, I sense someone close; it's a warmth nearby, and the hint of peanut butter and must.

"Can I try?" It's Donald, as usual.

"No! Wait till you get your own dog." Beauty's toy lands on my feet, and I pitch it again, high and far.

"When is your Mom buying one anyway?"

"Never. She says we don't have the money to feed an extra mouth."

"Gee, that's too bad." I feel sorry that I snapped at him and want to make everything better for him. "Listen, Donald, maybe you can talk to your mother about fostering a dog for Canine Vision Canada. You know, like Liz does? Then she wouldn't have to pay anything. They take care of food, vet fees, everything."

"Our landlord doesn't allow pets."

Beauty nudges my legs.

"Geez, you're back fast!" I sound like I'm mad at the

dog, but really, it's Donald's mom I'm annoyed with. Why would she promise the kid a dog when they weren't allowed to have one? I throw the toy much harder this time, and I hear it crash against a tree.

"We were supposed to move in with her boyfriend. He has a house. She said he'd get me a dog as long as I was nice. But they broke up."

Again, I want to say something to make him feel better. "You never know, they may get back together again."

"No! They can't. I hate him!"

I reach over and grab for his shoulder, just to pat it and make him know I care.

"Listen, Donald. Can you see if Beauty found the toy okay?"

"Yeah, she's on her way back."

"Good. Listen, I can't let you help me with Beauty, because I'm the only one who can play with her from now on."

"Sure, okay."

"But Elizabeth's going to come to the park with Magic. She doesn't mind if you throw the stick for her."

"Really?"

"Yup. And you know what you can help me with? I'm really hungry. Do you want to show Beauty and me the way to the doughnut shop? I'll let you pick one for yourself, too."

I know I can't fix Donald's world with a doughnut, but it helps him forget for a little while. We talk about all our favourite courtroom television shows. Donald really does want to be a lawyer; it has nothing to do with me whatsoever.

Next day at school, I put a copy of my essay along with the backup rough work on Mr. Veen's desk.

"I'll look at it, but I won't assign a grade," he tells me. "I told the whole class I wouldn't accept essays late. But go ahead and make your case with the office. They may give you special treatment."

I want to slug him, but I'd probably swing into empty space. Instead my fist opens and closes till I feel myself being yanked away.

"Let's go to the office," Maddie says.

"Forward, Beauty. "Maddie drags us off immediately, and, downstairs, starts to make my case with the vice principal, Mrs. Liu.

I interrupt. "I'm not asking for special treatment because I'm blind. I asked Mr. Veen for an extra week because I was sick. I can produce a doctor's letter."

Maddie hands Mrs. Liu one of the essays from my binder.

"Kyle turned in this essay today. It was due last Friday, so like he says, it's only a week late. Mr. Veen refuses to mark it. Most teachers would just deduct some marks, which would be fine. The essay is so good,

Kyle should still earn an A."

"All right. Leave this with me. I'll discuss this with Mr. Veen and let you know my conclusions."

Maddie won't just leave it with Mrs. Liu. She drags me to her favourite English teacher, Mrs. Dejean, and asks her to grade it.

"I can't second-guess another teacher. I'll look at it if Mrs. Liu asks me to."

We're on the ground floor, where most of the junior grades have their classes. Is Liz somewhere nearby, watching? I hesitate, listening, hoping, but without Beauty, she could be as close as my arms, and I would never know. I inhale, straining to smell that baby scent of hers, but it's impossible in the overwhelming school odours of bologna, socks and wet wool. Can I ask Maddie for help? I decide not to as she rushes me back to Veen's class.

Chapter 23

Elizabeth Alone

"I'm sorry, Alicia. But Scott's a two-timer. He always has been. You had to know this was going to happen."

"I didn't! People can change. And Scott told me he loved me."

"And you believed him." I roll my eyes, but luckily she can't see over the phone. "He probably said that so he could put the move on you at his uncle's chalet."

Alicia makes a little noise, like a suffocated mouse.

"Alicia? Alicia? Tell me you didn't fall for that line. Tell me it didn't work."

"It's not such a big deal. I'm glad I did it and got the first time over with. You're just as bad as I am, anyway. Tell me you're not in just as deep with Kyle."

"Alicia, nothing's happened between Kyle and me."

She chokes out another mouse noise. Alicia's the adventurous one, the boy magnet, the flirt, the one who has to do everything first. I sigh. Alicia's the one crying uncontrollably now, because she had no one to race against, and she still managed to lose something.

"You were careful, though, right?"

She makes a noise that sounds like yes and I sigh again. "Good. So you weren't that stupid."

"Stupid?" She blows up. "How is loving someone more than he loves you anything to do with brains? You're so smug—but your mother won't even let Kyle see you. You know that has to end badly, don't you? Who will be the stupid one then, huh?"

I can't listen to her anymore.

"Good bye, Alicia," I whisper and press the end button on the phone.

Over the click, I hear Teal calling out, "Bu, bu, bu." I walk past his room and call out, "Oh no you don't! Even if you're Einstein, you're not going to sucker me into changing the first diaper of the day."

I pound on Debra's door as I head past for the stairs.

Breakfast noises come from the kitchen. I smell bacon and see my mom flip a pancake. I set out the syrup and plates and, as fast as my parents swallow their first swig of coffee, I explain what I saw on the webcam. Mom immediately leaves a message on the Canine Vision voice mail, but it's Sunday. She'll have to confirm with them again on Monday.

"About this boy you're seeing," my mother begins.

Where is Deb when I need her? I wonder.

"We realize that we can't stop you from seeing him. We can't watch you twenty-four hours a day. But your new curfew is 10:00 on weekends. No sleepovers, since we can't trust you to actually be where you say you're going to be. During the week on school nights, we expect you to stay in."

"Am I still grounded?"

"Of course," Mom answers. "Two weeks."

"Good morning, all." Debra comes through the basement door carrying a gurgling Teal. "Just to let you know, Teal and I are moving in with Rolph today."

The doorbell rings. Magic barks. The toast pops. The coffeemaker beeps. I run for the door, with Magic galloping behind me. Surround sound chaos, as usual—a normal Sunday morning at the Kerr house.

Monday morning, though she's still not talking to me, Alicia messages me to let me know she's seen Kyle's ex go to his house on Sunday. I believe her.

I hate the way I feel, as if my insides have slid down into a hard clump at the pit of my stomach. He's told me over and over she's just a friend, but I'm still jealous.

Halfway through the morning, the puppy coordinator arrives to take Magic back, even after we explain why she's innocent of all biting charges. She thinks they might have spotted something on an X-ray, and they want to do something called a Pennhip Test. I'm not worried. I don't require genetic perfection the way Canine Vision does. If Magic flunks a hip test, she'll still be mine. Still, it's lonely to lose her even for a week. Especially today, when I have the whole day off but am not allowed to go anywhere.

Mom calls me after lunch and asks me what I'm doing.

I don't tell her that I'm in Teal's old room, staring up at the painted clouds on the ceiling. I sigh and tell her instead that I'm folding laundry, like she asked me to this morning.

"Mom, there are little tiny Teal socks in it."

"We'll see them on the weekend to return them."

"Everywhere I go, I find his toys. Mom, I miss him so much. And when he lived here, I thought he was just a pest."

"Mmm. Not too many people get to play that large a part in their nephew's life. Or their grandchild's, for that matter. We were lucky, and we didn't know it."

"Mom, what if he hits her?"

Tssssss. Like air going out of a tire. Mom can't say anything.

"I know she says he doesn't, but he still drinks—and lies."

"Liz, listen to me. This may be the hardest thing this family has ever gone through. But we have to be nice to

Rolph, so we stay in contact with Debra and Teal. Do you understand?"

I swallow hard and stare up at the cloud Debra painted into the shape of a dog. I don't understand. Why can't we do something?

"Liz, are you still there?"

"Uh huh."

"Go over to Alicia's house, if you like. I'll call you when I get home."

Escape! I take her up on it immediately, throwing on a coat and bursting through the door. The sun bounces back from the snow in blinding whiteness. I blink fast. Now what? I can't go to Alicia's—she's not talking to me. And I don't have a dog to walk.

My feet start swishing through the clumpy, wet snow. Maybe it will all melt soon, but it would be nice if the snow stayed for Christmas. I drift along, reaching out to catch the large, feathery snowflakes floating to the ground. I don't even know where I'm going, I just follow my feet till I'm at the park.

I hear his voice and see a dark silhouette against the snow. Kyle stands underneath some trees, quiet as his shadow. He seems all alone, the way I feel. How can he be here by himself? I wonder, so I approach him. He faces away from me, as though watching something or somebody, but of course he can't be. Then I see Beauty running free, ears flying back, legs outstretched, grin on her face. She's happier than I've seen her in a long time, and I wonder if I should just leave. I will have to decide quickly. When Beauty comes back, she'll let Kyle know I'm here for sure.

I call to him. Out here, we're alone together—I can get angry, and yell, and cry, and no one will know, maybe not even Kyle. How can he keep seeing Maddie and me at the same time? He's as bad as Scott.

Kyle reaches for me, and I don't want to melt.

"I know you had Maddie at your house Sunday."

"That was just my mother interfering again. She wants Maddie and me to go out, again. She just looked over my essay notes and left. But you're the only person I want to go out with. Let's make it official."

He drops to one knee and holds my hand. His eyes shine optimistically up at the winter sky.

What about Beauty? And my mother, and our age, and a million other things? I think—but then I know I can't say no. I'm so alone, and I look at Kyle and believe in love again. I swallow hard and finally tell him something I've held back since the first day I met him.

"I love you."

Chapter 24

Kyle and Beauty

That night I call Liz's mom. I don't know what to say to make her feel better about me, but I try everything. I promise her I won't come to the house when Liz is alone. I promise I won't have her over when I'm alone. I promise I'll never do anything to hurt Liz. I feel like I could keep any promise as long as Liz can be in my life.

I ask her to look at my essay, explain that Mr. Veen won't mark it, and that the other teachers won't grade it without an official okay. Then I tell her the one thing I haven't admitted out loud to another adult. I'm not even sure why I confess.

"Mrs. Kerr, I cheated on his pop quiz. It was a stupid thing to do. The thing wasn't even worth that much. I just didn't want him to think I couldn't handle the workload."

"Hmm. Well, I believe you. Why don't you bring your

paper over tomorrow? You can see Elizabeth at the same time."

What? I can't believe my ears. I'm getting another chance. "Thank you, thank you. I'll bring it to you after school."

And I do. I take the bus with Donald. First, we get off at the park, to let Beauty play for a bit. I'm feeling strange, sluggish, like I've been inside too long. There's pressure on my chest, like a weight is sitting there.

Donald forgets about what I told him yesterday and wants to pitch the toy for Beauty all over again. Because my arm feels a bit numb, I almost want to let him.

"Sorry. I can't, buddy. The dog has to answer to me alone, remember? You can walk with us, though."

We head down the same path as Liz and I rollerbladed earlier.

"Whoa, look at the stream. It's all frozen over. They never let us play on the ice around the school." Donald stomps along, crunching down patches of snow and ice.

I smile. I remember the sensation of banging my heel into the white part of the ice, watching it splinter open. If I could see to find the weak spots, I'd be chiselling at it myself today; at least I would if I felt a little stronger.

"Do you want to come play on the stream with me?" Donald asks.

Another sensation I remember, my feet sliding across the hard slipperiness. Almost always, I would end up falling on my butt—but those few seconds of effortless glide were worth it. I don't need my sight for that; I could join Donald, but I feel too heavy and can't muster the energy.

"Not today. I'm not feeling that great."

"Okay." Donald's voice is already far away. He's heading down the stream bank, by the sounds of it.

"Hey, Kyle," he calls, "there's a rabbit on the other side."

In my head, I picture it. I love the way, when they're startled, they spring away, powder-puff tail in salute. When I was ten years old, I chased them just the way I know Donald will.

"Be careful!" I call to him. I reach down to pat Beauty and feel her ears at attention. Her body is stiff and poised to chase, too.

"Good girl, Beauty," I tell her. Like the perfect dog guide she is, she's resisting. Suddenly, I hear a thump, and almost at the same time a panicky, scared cry. "Ow, ouch!"

"Donald, what's wrong? Are you all right?"

"I fell. My arm hurts!"

Crick, crick, crick. Strange sounds; I think hard about what they mean. "Donald, get out of there. Fast!" I shout to him.

"I'm trying." *Slosh, slosh*. "The ice cracked!" Donald's voice turns high-pitched, younger.

"I can't get out. Kyle, I'm stuck!"

"Take it easy, Donald." My voice comes out high-pitched, too. I've got to get a grip, for his sake. But damn it, I can't see to help him.

What am I going to do? How can I find him? I pitch my backpack and wrestle in my pocket for my cell phone.

"Listen, Donald, look around and tell me if you see anyone else."

"It's dark out."

I punch in the emergency number.

"Hello, yes." I speak into the receiver now. "Can you send someone to Little Stone Bridge Park? A boy's fallen through the ice."

"The water's ss-so cc-cold!" Donald chatters, then moans.

"Hold on. Help is on the way. Five minutes, tops." Only... how long can someone little last in such cold water?

"The water's pulling. I can't hold on."

I shiver all over. I'm so useless. How can I help Donald? I have to try.

"I'm coming. Hang on," I yell.

"Forward, Beauty. Down to the stream. Fast." I jog to give Beauty the idea but lose my breath as I run. An elephant crushes my chest with each step. The anxiety has exploded into a blaze surrounding my heart.

"Tell me where you are," I call as my feet stutter down

the sloping bank towards the water.

"Over here. I'm in the middle."

The middle part of the stream is the deepest. I've never seen Donald, to know how tall he is, exactly, but the water's got to be over his head there—can I make it in time? I stumble onto a hard surface and hear cracking immediately.

"Find Donald, Beauty."

Donald's crying now.

"Keep talking to me. I'm coming."

But the ice gives beneath my feet, and a shock of bitter cold water bites at my ankle and shin bone. Across my chest, lightning zigzags.

I lift one leg then the other, crashing through the ice behind Beauty. How deep will it get?

"Hurry, Kyle."

Donald sounds as if he's only a few metres from me. My feet breaking through the ice feel as though they're shattering glass. Ice splinters up my pant legs and finds a way to stab into my chest. The water sucks at me, too. It's at my thigh now, but with each crash through the ice, it becomes higher and harder to make the next step. The current pulls me like a herd of icy horses.

"How far are you? Can you see me?"

"Yes," he calls back weakly.

I stumble and fall but can't get up any more. Maybe spreading my weight across the ice will keep it from breaking. Instead, I reach up to grab Beauty's harness and crawl towards the sound of Donald's voice. As I move forward, my knees slip out from under me, and I fall to my chin. I have to crawl slower, one hand on the ice, the other still high gripping the leather. The ice sinks behind me as fast as I lift my knee.

"Find him, girl. Find Donald."

"I'm right here." He touches me, and I grab his hand.

I pull as hard as I can but don't budge him. Instead, the ice beneath me cracks.

Donald cries out.

I put his hand on Beauty's tail.

"Hold on to her, Donald. We'll get you out."

Still on my knees, I manoeuvre to pound and smash all around his body, trying to find the weak points in the ice. Water rises up over my arm. Donald doesn't talk anymore.

"Pull, Beauty. Donald? Donald?" No answer. I stoop lower and fumble for his body, wrapping one arm around him. I pull him up higher and wrap my other arm around Beauty.

"Forward." She hauls us up, even as I feel ice give way. Water seeps around.

"Keep going, girl," I tell Beauty. I crawl onto a firmer patch, dragging Donald along side me.

It happens over and over again. As fast as I get to the next piece of ice, we sink down.

"Pull, Beauty." She manages to drag me and Donald up and forward as the water sucks around my ankles.

I force myself to breathe as we inch toward the bank. I don't know how far we have left to go, I don't know if I can hold out. I just know to trust Beauty.

Then I hit hard earth with my knee and heave Donald up on the slope of dry ground. I climb up after him, ripping off my jacket to cover him.

"Talk to me. Talk to me. Oh, my God, please talk to me."

Another shock of pain explodes across my chest, and I find it impossible to breathe. But I hear his voice.

"I'm cold."

Did I imagine that? I pick him up and hold him close to get him warm, so close and tight that I can feel his heartbeat. He is alive; we're both out of the water and ice. I try to breathe, but I can't get hold of the air.

A siren screams at us from far away. The scream becomes louder and I'm glad.

"Don't worry, Donald," I try to say, but nothing will come out. The squad car will be warm. Donald will be all right and, maybe in there, I'll be able to breathe again. The screaming stops.

"Here, I'll take him." A man's voice, and then Donald is lifted from me. I collapse on the hard, cold ground. Something white shatters and splinters through me. What is happening to me? The white bursts behind my eyelids. I feel myself lifting, lifting.

I open my eyes. It seems like hours later, and I can see bright colours, green trees and grass, blue water and skies, white clouds, a huge yellow yolk of a sun. I know by the incredible warmth inside me that this is a whole different time and place. In my arms, a baby with a tuft of autumn-coloured hair gurgles at me. He has flecks of dark brown in golden eyes, but he's too young to be Teal.

I feel such a strong bond of love towards him that I understand he is my own son.

Where's Beauty? No dog, anywhere, but as I look around I realize I can see. I don't need a dog guide. This has to be a dream; but I can smell the grass and the fresh air, and I never smell things in my dreams. A girl in her early twenties smiles at me and holds out her hands for the baby.

Across her nose is a sprinkle of freckles. She has the same eyes as the baby, and long, curly, autumn-coloured hair. In the distance, I hear a voice calling my name, a voice I love, like chimes in the wind. But Liz is here. Why would I go back when everything I ever wanted is here? I kiss this Liz—older, more perfect—and we walk away together into our future.

Chapter 25

Elizabeth and Beauty

"What do you mean, Magic's not coming back?"

My mother explains it to me in her patient, super-slow teacher's voice. "The problem in Magic's hip is significant enough to disqualify for breeding but not as a dog guide."

"I don't even get to say goodbye?" I whisper.

My mother shakes her head. "She's old enough to begin training. She doesn't need a foster family anymore."

A punch in the stomach—her words make me double up and hold myself in pain.

"Every time I raise a dog, I end up loving it and then having to give it up. It's not fair."

It's not fair, the little kid in me echoes. The adult answers, *Life's not fair*. I suddenly feel too adult. Like there's no hope, like everything always ends up badly.

"It wasn't supposed to happen this way. No one could have predicted the hip problem."

I look away from her face, so I can hold back the tears. The trouble is, wherever I look, there's some sign of Magic: her crate in the corner, her water and food dishes by the cupboards and in the hall, her stuffed animal. Wait a minute, maybe that belongs to Teal. I swallow hard over that one, too.

"Maybe this will cheer you up a little..." my mother continues. "Kyle is coming over with an essay for me to mark. I'm going to look at it and maybe talk to Allan Veen about it. You see, I am getting to know your friend, giving him a chance the way you asked me to."

"I don't want Kyle. I want my dog." I don't mean that, of course. I'm just so mad. I mean I want everything. I want Deb and Teal back, Magic, and Kyle, and Beauty. I don't want to give up anybody in my life.

In my mind, I hear Magic barking. I shake my head but still hear her. It's so loud; frantic, desperate even. She's howling like a wolf and scratching at the door.

"What is that?" my mother asks. She must hear her, too. It's not just in my head.

I run to the front door and yank it open. "Beauty?" She's standing there white-eyed, her mouth hanging open, foam dripping from it. Her fur looks wet, but she's still wearing her harness, the handle empty.

"Beauty, where is Kyle? You didn't leave him?"

Inside, I know the answer. Beauty would have never left Kyle unless... A horrible, cold feeling shudders through me.

"Mom, something's wrong!" I grab my coat, and Mom follows me as I take Beauty's harness. Beauty gallops, and I fly behind her. We run so hard and long, my gums throb.

As we near the park, I see an ambulance careen out from the jogging path. There's also a flashing ribbon of lights from a police car parked in the parking lot. Mom grabs my hand as we follow Beauty down to the dark shape of a tree near the stream. Beauty is pawing at something on the ground amongst the leaves—Kyle's backpack. I pick it up and wrap my fingers round the handle. I feel Kyle's presence and call out his name, thinking he's got to be okay, but then the sensation ebbs away.

Mom puts her arms around me and pulls my head into her shoulder.

She strokes the back of my head.

"We'll call Kyle's parents. There's no point worrying over anything when we just don't know."

But somewhere, deep down inside, I do know. Something awful is wrong with Kyle. Over her shoulder, I see a policeman with a flashlight approaching us.

"That your dog?" he shouts.

"No. Yes."

He ignores me and talks to my mom. "Paramedics reported a dog on the loose. Is that the one?"

"Yes," I answer. "She's a dog guide. She belonged to Kyle."

I hear the past tense, the hollowness of Kyle's name without his presence. It's like the empty harness sticking out from Beauty's back.

Packed into the church are rows and rows of kids from school, the band members, the school council—Alicia's in there, third row back—and the vice principal and principal. There are people with dog guides, too. Ahead of me, Angela sits with her Golden Retriever, Butterscotch. She and Butterscotch trained together with Kyle and Beauty, and we met them at Dog Guides Canada graduation last summer.

Squeezed between parents, Donald looks so young and sad that I want to cry for him, too. Ryan, sitting closer to the front, dressed in a suit, looks as pale and hollow as I feel. Beside him, Maddie hides her head in her folded arms, which lie across the pew ahead of her. All their sorrow keeps pressing down on me so heavy that my ribs hurt, my heart aches. They make this bad dream into something too real.

I'm going to be sick again. I close my eyes tightly, hold my stomach, and swallow. I look down at Beauty lying at my feet. Something in her sad eyes keeps me going.

"You have to be strong, for her sake," my mother told me yesterday, when Canine Vision called and asked us to pick up Beauty. They'd never seen such a broken-hearted dog. They were hoping that I could love her enough for her spirit, at least, to return. I couldn't forget the sight of Beauty in the kennel, head and eyes down. When I called to her and her tail barely flapped once, I started to cry and couldn't stop.

We're at the back of the church and I don't want Mrs. Nicholson to hear me crying. I don't want to upset her even more. I've never seen an adult cry the way she does. It's as if someone is ripping out her soul.

Beauty whines and shifts herself beside me. I reach down and pat her, and she licks my hand. Canine Vision told us I could finally keep a dog. They couldn't retrain Beauty; she was too attached to me after losing Kyle. Even that feels awful, like something bad that I wished for came true.

I look up again and, through a blur, see the agonizingly bright colours of the stained glass windows.

I look forward again. It's hard because then I have to face the coffin with his picture on it. Kyle, with his optimistic eyes, always staring in one direction—upwards. One red rose lies across the coffin—the one I bought this morning. Everyone else donated money to the Diabetes Foundation. The minister says that our high school alone donated five thousand dollars. Good, maybe they'll figure out some way for blood-sugar testing not to hurt so much. Kyle would like that.

I see Shawna standing between her father, straight and tall, and her mother, bowed over. She's holding her mother and her father's hands. Is she trying not to cry, too? She's doing a far better job than I am.

The minister talks about how Kyle's quick thinking saved Donald from fatal hypothermia. My mother explained to me that Kyle had a heart defect; undetected despite all the medical attention he received for diabetes. The stress and exertion of the rescue brought on the heart attack, but it might have happened at any other time, too—just bad luck.

Bad luck that he had diabetes, bad luck that he went blind from it, bad luck that in saving a boy from drowning, his own heart gave out—but was that bad luck? For sure, Kyle would be happier knowing he died while saving Donald rather than randomly dying while, say, Rollerblading in the park or surfing in Waikiki. How many people save a life, even if they live to be a hundred?

The minister says Kyle has gone to a better place. Well, he can't have just disappeared and gone into nothingness. That can't be what death is all about.

Angela walks forward with Butterscotch and a guitar. She introduces a song that she and Kyle wrote about their dog guides. She sings, and the lyrics open up another ache inside me—part of his life I never knew. So much we could have learned together. Her voice sounds like a violin singing the words. I bet Kyle liked her.

The minister invites people to stand up and say things in a testimony to the life Kyle lived. I try to think of something.

Beside my mother, Mr. Veen stands up.

"Kyle Nicholson was a stubborn student who refused to back down from a challenge. He was also a terrific writer, insightful and sensitive. So much so, I could never believe the writing was his own. I'm sorry, Kyle." Lame words, and too late to help anyone; except, they seem to give others courage, or maybe just time to think of things to say. Other people start to rise from their seats.

"He loved driving my Mustang with the top down. He was a better driver than my sister." Ryan makes Mrs. Nicholson smile for a moment, and I forgive him for all the stupid things he's ever said to me.

A guy I saw at Ryan's party stands. "Kyle taught me some tricky fingering on the guitar. He wrote lots of his own songs. I thought he had a lot of talent."

Maddie lifts her head and stands. "He worked ten times harder on his schoolwork than anyone else. He wanted to go to Queens and be a lawyer like his dad." In the front row, his father buckles in his chair, and Shawna wraps her arms around him.

I want to do something to make him and Kyle's mother feel better. What, though? The answer comes to me as a melody in my head. I tap Angela on the shoulder and ask her to come up with me.

We stand near the minister, till Beauty whines and pulls me to the coffin. I call Angela, and she tells Butterscotch to find Beauty. Now we're both close to Kyle, even though I feel that, really, he's very far away.

I clear my throat.

"Kyle wanted to be..." I clear my throat again and swallow hard. "Kyle would have been a great dad. He once held my nephew Teal when he was sick, and sang this song to him."

I whisper the name of it into Angela's ear, and she begins to strum. I miss the whole verse before I can find my voice to start.

Sunshine and starlight
Reflect in your eyes
When you smile at me baby,
The clouds leave the skies

Angela's voice joins me, and after another few lines Shawna sings, too.

The world can be a dark place
Full of thunder, full of rain,

Life can bring hardship,
Love can bring pain

More voices join us. It's impossible to tell for sure, but it looks as if Kyle's mom is singing, or at least mouthing the words.

But I will love you always
You can close your sweet eyes
And I'll protect you baby
Till once again you rise

I close my eyes, and Angela keeps strumming as she starts through the song again. In my mind, I hear Kyle singing. He's looking down at a baby in his arms. Teal? I swallow hard. He's in a better place, I tell myself, because that's the only thing I can believe. Beauty whines softly at my feet, and I bend down to hug her. She's all I have left of him. Beauty licks the tears from my face, and I sing the lullaby again, this time to her.

We're the last ones left at the graveside, Alicia and I. I told Mom we would walk home later. Alicia hugs me and cries into my shoulder.

"I'm so sorry. When I said it would end badly for you, I never dreamt that...this could happen."

"That's okay. Nobody did." My voice comes out flat. I

can't feel anything, anger, or forgiveness, or sadness, or pain.

Beauty whines loudly and slumps to the ground. Suddenly I feel as if all my insides have been heaved up.

"It will be all right," I choke out to Beauty and Alicia. Something I learned from all the worst, scariest, saddest times in my life—in the end, things always turn out all right. Something I can't believe just right now, but I can tell them, and maybe it will be true.

Alicia breaks off a sob. "What are we going to do?"

I wipe at my face too, now. "The same thing we always do."

I look at Alicia and try to smile, "Swear off boys."

Beauty agrees. She starts barking and wags her tail.

"You're right. This time we really have to do it."

She hugs me long and hard, then pulls away, blows her nose, and looks in my face.

"At least for a long, long while."

THE END